Justine Delaney Wilson

Listen for the Weather

HACHETTE
BOOKS
IRELAND

First published in Ireland in 2018 by
HACHETTE BOOKS IRELAND

3

Cataloguing in Publication Data is available from the British Library

ISBN 9781473625921

Typeset in Century Old Style by redrattledesign.com

Printed and bound in Great Britain by Clays Ltd, St Ives plc

Excerpt from *Why Be Happy When You Could Be Normal?*, copyright © 2011 by
Jeanette Winterson. Used by permission of Grove/Atlantic, Inc. Any third party use of
this material, outside of this publication, is prohibited.
Excerpt from *Why Be Happy When You Could Be Normal?* by Jeanette Winterson,
published by Jonathan Cape, reprinted by permission of
The Random House Group Limited. © 2011
'The Beadsman' by C.P. Stewart, from *Considering the Lilies*. Copyright 2011 by estate
of C.P. Stewart. Reprinted by permission of Wordsonthestreet

Hachette Books Ireland policy is to use papers that are natural, renewable and
recyclable products and made from wood grown in sustainable forests. The logging and
manufacturing processes are expected to conform to the environmental regulations of
the country of origin.

Hachette Books Ireland
8 Castlecourt Centre
Castleknock
Dublin 15, Ireland

A division of Hachette UK Ltd
Carmelite House, 50 Victoria Embankment, EC4Y 0DZ

www.hachettebooksireland.ie

To Morgan, Reuben and Lily-Rose,
for all the reasons

There are times when it will go so wrong that you will barely be alive, and times when you realise that being barely alive, on your own terms, is better than living a bloated half-life on someone else's terms.

Jeanette Winterson, *Why Be Happy When You Could be Normal?*

October 2017

We stand either side of the kettle and watch the water boil. The milk carton on the counter has Steve's birth date along the top. He will be fifty in four days' time, the same day that this milk will expire. We're having a party for him on Saturday night. Here, in our home, with our friends and neighbours. A celebration! This very weekend.

'I just don't know – I don't know what to do. I can't get my head around it.' His voice is quiet, his words rushed. 'How can this— I mean, it was so long ago. Barely a memory now.'

My husband is standing with me, the steam from a boiled kettle between us, recalling a night of sex with another woman during our marriage. Remembering it, unearthing the details, scrambling for clues. I watch him through the damp cloud. My mind spools. I think about our son, our daughter. I steady myself against the back of a chair. And then something drops from my jawbone and I find I'm crying. The way a little child might.

I am longing to be with you, and by the sea, where we can talk together freely and build our castles in the air.

Bram Stoker, *Dracula*

One week earlier

My mother finishes cleaning her fridge on the other side of the world. Then she empties the contents of the washing machine into the laundry basket and starts to hang them – a handful of tiny things. Underwear.

'I like to clear it as it builds up, Beth. To keep ahead,' she says loudly into the room. 'You should get into that habit.'

She hunches over the table and her face fills my laptop screen. The skin around her eyes is slick and pale, the lines of age and stress luscious with just-applied cream.

'Oh, yes, I knew there was something I had to tell you.' Her clipped voice speaks from her kitchen in Dublin and resonates in mine, here in New Zealand. 'I saw your old neighbour Moirah in the car park at the supermarket. She was scolding her son. Didn't know I was watching her, of course.' My mother's words are full of tone.

She moves on to prising open a jar.

'It turns out she has a tongue that could burst a balloon. I must say I was very surprised. She's always so put-together.'

I sit, engaged by the stubbornness of the lid, not caring about Moirah or her son or any of the put-together others we left behind in the desiccating routines of Vesey Hill, or dwelling on the fact that my mother could be describing herself.

She holds the jar under the hot tap, then goes to work on it with pincers. We are both quiet now. The lid is everything.

Silence across the miles as I stare and my mother grimaces. Then the jar yields to her will and opens. She brushes at her forehead with the back of her hand, satisfied. Dramatic. Now there's space for us to speak.

'Did you get the card Mae sent you?' I say, to avoid more non-gossip about old neighbours.

'Oh, yes, with some sort of a strange house drawn on the front. Lovely.'

'That's a *marae*. A Maori ancestral home. She was learning about them at school.'

'Oh, I see. Well, that's nice.'

'I think you might like to visit one,' I say. And then I come over all tourist board, the way I do when I speak to my parents. 'The Maori believe in valuing each person and their ancestors.' I can't seem to stop myself. 'They're very welcoming to outsiders.'

'Isn't it well for them! Sounds like they've nothing to do all day. I'd never find the time for that. I can barely welcome the people I do know.'

That's true.

'I'll speak to your father and look into the idea, but to be honest, Beth, I don't think we'll bother with this – this *marae.*' She dismisses it with her hand, shaking the idea of it off her fingers.

Over the past year or so, she has been scrupulously picking through all the places she and my father will go and the running order for each day when they arrive here on the trip that will never happen.

'It might give him something to think about, though. He hasn't been in very good form since he reversed his car into the wall in the garden yesterday. He said that the thing – you know, the sensor thing – didn't beep. But I mean, honestly,' she bends over to pick something up, a piece of fluff, perhaps, from the carpet, and her voice drops out as she does, 'we've been here long enough.' Her voice rises again as her face looms large on the screen. 'You'd think he'd know where the boundaries are by now.'

I smile.

'I told him that this is precisely the kind of thing that you can expect when you come to rely on technology. Of course, he pretended to be listening to me. Much like you are now, darling.'

My parents can't imagine our lives. They confuse the move, our freedom, with recklessness. Leaving our beautiful home in a prestigious suburban housing estate with measured-out hours and days, in favour of what my mother gravely calls 'sunshine and lifestyle'. It's nothing more than a dropping out of reality, middle-aged foolishness. Her friends frown and shake their heads with her.

And I can't explain the containment of our old life to her. The cult of home improvements and order. The unnerving lack of *sensation*. I can't articulate it well enough to make her hear me. But, then, I've always been useless around my mother, a hollowed-out version of myself. I'm even physically lumbering and incapable when she's in the room. I can't iron in a straight line if I think she's watching. But she doesn't know that it's just her watchful presence that disables me. That I'm not so entirely helpless when she isn't there to see. So she wonders, perhaps not unreasonably, how I survive, how I get anything done.

However do you manage things, Beth?

When we speak, I think she sounds as far away as she is. Oceans away.

And I don't get much of a chance to describe our life to my father. We don't speak a lot any more. He gives a little salute into the camera as he passes, bellows a clownish hello at my children, Al and Mae. Occasionally he'll stop to ask me about the weather here. Then he'll check the app on his phone to corroborate what I've said.

As far as he's concerned, only slackers expect to enjoy their lives.

Slackers, and him.

I've wanted to shout at him for a long time. I never have, though.

Sometimes I'll feel a memory suddenly, like a slap – my father advising me on my wedding day in the heat of the Spanish sun, mopping at his brow and telling me not to set the bar too high, how nobody can ever really make promises, and I shouldn't think that somehow Steve and I can, promises only leading to disappointment.

Years after this, I learned of his affair. An affair. One, or one of many? Who can tell?

And who would want to think about that anyway?

I boxed up and stored away the knowledge of it, of promises made to my mother now broken, of my own disappointment in him and in love. My father. I haven't stayed quiet about it to preserve the peace – the gentleness of peace isn't theirs – but rather to preserve their glassy silence. It isn't mine to break.

He doesn't know I saw him that evening, leaning into Gloria in the darkness of the golf club car park, his arms around her under her cashmere coat, her hair loose and wild across her shoulders. He'll never know I saw him, his polished shoe catching our car's lights as we passed.

He had tried to warn me. Kind of.

My mother has lived her life smiling too brightly, hiding her various hurts, turning her earring in its lobe and looking the other way. Love chooses not to see, chooses to ignore what doesn't suit it.

I'm glad to be away from it all. And I'm as far away as possible. If I was any further down the globe, I'd be on my way back up. I live my life differently, knowing they aren't watching, knowing I can't watch them. And it feels good, like cycling without holding on.

We say our awkward goodbyes and my mother ends the call.

I breathe out, feeling further from her than I did before I rang.

I suspect she does too.

* * *

Some spring mornings, like this one, it feels warm when I waken. The days are already generous with their time. It will be summer soon, another Christmas. The holly wreaths and fairy lights will hide in the brightness of the long evenings and the bursting blooms of the trees.

It's a change from the months of festive mayhem I knew in Dublin. That circus of distraction starting in October, turning our heads from the bleak winter and dragging us into the new year towards brighter showers of February, via the stacked mess of rails in the January sales. Scuttling along for weeks, dark mornings and afternoons, shopping and eating, until something catches the dead light – the first clump of golden daffodils bold as brass and there to save us.

Our first day here was in December, nearly three years ago. Like four birds, we had flown south from Ireland to escape the cold. And all the shopping. The warmth eased the frost from us – the trees awash with the light of early mornings, and the late-evening skies a deep pink as the sun reluctantly bowed out for the night.

My son Alex had no associations when we arrived, which suited him at sixteen. Starting out. Breaking out. No old childhood cliques and schoolyard history to shrink to fit any more. He gained a freedom in New Zealand that he hadn't known he'd lacked. Being physically dwarfed by the mountains and the sea made him feel small and separate from old things. Took him out of his head.

'I never understood that expression before, you know? "I'm out of my head." But I do now,' he said. 'And it's good.' And then, after a pause, 'Sweet as.'

He is nineteen now and plans to study art at college next year. He has a new girlfriend, Lisa. 'We're together but I'm in it all the way up to my ankles, so don't worry, Mum.' He smiles, and doesn't look like himself any more. Or maybe it's that he does – for the first time.

He's already better at being an adult than he ever was at being a child. Those years spent trying to be less serious, kicking a ball and applying himself to being carefree, like the others, as if that was how it worked. Now, the world is opening up for him and he feels his place in it. He is happy.

My daughter Mae is asleep in the shade of the tree on our lawn. She is lying on her side, legs and arms stretched out in front of her as though she fell to the ground so relaxed that she sank into it. She will always have associations, ties. Her face gives her away. Down syndrome. But here, at least, she is warm to the touch. Not mottled and cold, living a half-life in a damp country. She rides her bike all year round now.

I can feel her contentment lying there – her arms open to the world, her crescent eyelids closed making two still and tiny smiles. The tip of her white-faded scar peeks out at the neck of her T-shirt, a heart surgery from before. Before we left. It changes colour to a line of blush in the water when she swims, which is most days now. It has lost its teeth, this scar. I see it as a mark of courage and strength. Mostly.

'You're so lucky she had citizenship,' my neighbour Moirah had said, when we were leaving Dublin. 'Very lucky. That she had it automatically, because of her dad.' I'd said nothing as she explained my own family circumstances to me. 'They don't allow you in if they think – well, you know – that you're going to be a drain on the country.'

This brown-eyed girl. Draining a country. Imagine it.

From our front garden, I see the harbour lights at the end of the hill, our street sloping down to reassuring waters. The tops of the sails are flags marking the blue of the Pacific Ocean meeting the Tasman Sea. I have confidence in us, here. I had suspected there could be a life like this, an ease and a freedom. Steve had told me, and the enchantment in his face when he spoke of it was contagious.

The first time he and I walked to the beach at the end of

this road. The salt taste on his mouth when my face tilted to meet it. We would thrive here in the sea air. This would be our real beginning, the past dragged out of sight by the endless pull of the waves. Pulling things away, pulling the weight of my old life from me.

I never look about me and wonder what I'm doing here. This white wooden house, with its wrap-around porch and giant swing, feels like the best version of us, a place where we talk. The cinder bowl of Mount Eden behind us has our back, gives us shelter.

And I'm writing again, like I did years ago. Before Mae, before shock, before. I work part-time as a copywriter, and I write stories and poetry of my own. And all of it feels like a moving forward – even more than that: it feels like a little uprising. My days full of *sensation*.

To wish for nothing more than your own life, as it is. Who would've known there was such a feeling?

I walk around the side of our house now, lifting the latch on the wooden gate. The glowing coals from the barbecue move shadows across Steve's hands. Hands that felt my desire for change and took me away from what I knew. Their form is seductive to me still. The past few years have been altitude training for our marriage: no supports, nothing familiar, Steve and I stripped back and leaning on each other, getting through, facing only forward.

Our lives put through a sieve, with only the gems remaining after the shake.

Hearing the gate, he looks up. He is holding tongs, and waves a piece of chicken. Our meals seem to taste of sunshine here, the sun plumping the food, drawing out the flavours, our plates a riot of juice and colour.

Steve is no longer a visitor. His feet are back on his land, so he feels comfortable and sure of himself. My connection is recent, a blink, not enriched by stories or generations. But I like that. I have no history with this new place, no hang-ups, no inheritance – other than it being a part of my children's make-up. A world of different places with strange names and poetic sounds – Aramoana, Whitianga, Rotorua. I don't feel dislocated. Being an outsider in a foreign land is preferable to being an outsider in my homeland.

I'm a ball shot from a cannon that has cleared the smallness of old routines. So I'm exiled but, also, I belong. I do. I belong among the pohutukawa trees with their blood-vivid blossoms in the spring sun. Following their pattern, the clear changing of the seasons. You know where you are when there are distinct seasons.

The smell of food and charcoal hangs in the air and I overhear some of the conversation. Al is in the swing chair on the back deck, his voice carrying: 'It's not all marshmallows on fondue forks when you're camping properly, you know, Dad.'

Steve's pushing a lime wedge into the neck of a beer bottle. 'See? Like this,' he says to Al, his voice rosy with beer and happiness. The lime squirts into his eye. Steve laughs and rubs his face, then stretches his arms high and leans back, listening to Al's chatter, taking the words in, making room for them. He is generous in conversations with me too, enthusiastic to listen. It's a sea of difference from the bitty, sulky exchanges he and I had grown used to. The silences and misunderstandings have been left behind. Perhaps they're in our house in Dublin, stored in one of the many cardboard boxes. Old sorrow and betrayal seeping from the attic into the lives of the family renting our rooms below.

This is where my life happens. Mountains to street to sea.

No boxes.

'Bring your bags, leave your baggage,' my friend Sommer had said.

Mae is awake now, standing by the barbecue, sleepily scratching her nose. Her cheeks are full of colour and a band of freckles crosses her forehead. She is seven. The age of reason for children. In the normal run of things.

Steve hunkers down to her level, speaks quietly to her.

'Can I play now, Mama?' She turns to me, her eyes suddenly wide. 'Can I? Before food?'

The Kiwi accent that swept around her soft words soon after we arrived here has settled in.

Teeny Wahine, Steve calls her.

I nod.

She turns back. 'Okay, Dad.' She gives him a little thumbs-up and sets off across the lawn.

The muscles in his calves form hard rectangles as he runs after her. She throws her head back and laughs, her open mouth showing tiny straight teeth. 'Twenty-one teeth,' she told us proudly after her first visit to the dentist last week. She held a little mirror and counted them along with him, his tiny mirror touching each one in turn. She sat up sideways on the big seat, her legs dangling – no reclining in this strange room. He had taken off his mask and put it into a drawer when she'd looked at it, stared at it. Such small kindnesses smooth over her worries and keep her happy.

So I am happy too.

I have a good friend here, a new friend, I suppose – Claire. She and I had been told of each other many times before we met. Someone else with a child of the same age who also has an extra chromosome, which, to be fair, is pretty common ground between us, as it's not common at all in Auckland. It means we both gather a lot of acquaintances as we go about our days. Claire and I encounter a lot of people who recognise us, who remember our faces. By association with our daughters' faces.

We first met after setting up a play-date for our children over the phone. I wasn't sure if it was a terrible idea or a great one so I'd decided to get her number and make the call, in case Mae saw her own image reflected, in case she felt something she'd been missing. A kindred. A part of herself as yet unmet. We didn't describe ourselves or our daughters during that call, what we would be wearing, where exactly we would be sitting. Distinctive features are easily seen.

So, Claire and I had a blind date of our own on a bench, while both girls hovered and spoke a little, hovered, and then parted ways to opposite sides of the playground. We watched them watch each other from the safety of distance. And we gave it time, gave them time.

Perhaps Mae and Georgia did see each other mirrored back through their almond eyes and didn't like it; perhaps they did feel something and it was uncomfortable or didn't seem right; perhaps they didn't see or feel anything. I was doing enough feeling that day for all of us. But, whatever the reason, they were repelled by each other that afternoon, like two equally charged magnets. And nothing has changed between them since.

Claire and I stood smiling at them both before we all left on that first day.

'She has a funny voice,' Mae said, in her own soft tone, an observation, a confusion. Used to hearing this said about herself. Never being the one to say it before.

Georgia stayed silent, presumably used to hearing it too.

In spite of the tangle of associations, Claire and I became friends. Initially, our friendship broke unfamiliar ground for me: I was unaccustomed to being the mother with the more able daughter – the one who mixed more easily, was beginning to read quite well and could be, often, understood. I didn't know whether to feel proud or apologetic. I saw more clearly than ever how easy it is for people to say the wrong thing.

When we met this morning, Claire told me about her weekend with her husband, Pete. Their first break away without their children – without Georgia – in more than four years. 'It must be twenty miles long, the beach where we sat. And then a man comes up, seemingly out of nowhere, carrying a bucket and spade. A grown man, alone. And he sits right next to us. The entire beach is empty, and he practically sits on top of us. I'm not joking, Beth. I just thought, For fuck's sake, is this guy for real? So Pete turns to say something to him and I look at him properly and, in the same moment, we both see he has Down syndrome. And we say nothing. I can't get anything out. I turned away from his eyes, from his face.' She runs her hand through her hair, is silent for a minute. 'I actually looked away and said nothing, Beth. Can you believe that? I did exactly what I hate people doing when they notice Georgia.'

I can believe it. I would probably have done the same.

'Anyway, he starts building sandcastles, right there, next to us. The rest of the beach is absolutely deserted – I'm not exaggerating now, there wasn't a soul anywhere – and this guy is making sandcastles next to Pete and me, beaming at us and looking for our encouragement. It was so familiar. The set of his mouth as he smiled, all hopeful. And, fuck, I just wanted to get up and run. To take Pete's hand and run. To get out of there. But I couldn't leave the guy. There wasn't anybody around keeping an eye on him, waiting to see him home. Nobody taking responsibility. It nearly sent me over the edge, I'm not joking. I'd love to say it felt meaningful or something. Like a sign. Or that I smiled at him, was kind, chatted with him. But I didn't. Neither of us did. We just sat it out until eventually he got up and left.

'It completely freaked me out,' she said quietly. 'It was as if my future found me, miles away, on my one day off, and sat down next to me to play in the sand.' She stopped talking.

'Same life, different beach,' I said uselessly, as a place-holder, in the absence of something more positive coming to mind.

'Pete was off form for the rest of the afternoon and neither of us brought it up. We do enough of that kind of talking every other day.' She paused for a minute, then looked at me. 'The ghost of our fucking future, you know?'

I didn't know if she meant *our* future, hers and mine, or *our* future, hers and Pete's. I'd thought I'd left those feelings behind me. That cage. I put my hand on hers, and hoped it didn't seem patronising, like it did when other mothers did it to me.

It's getting late and we're still in the garden. Mae has curled herself among a nest of cushions on the swing chair. Al's girlfriend Lisa is here now too. The five of us are lit by a citronella glow. Steve and I are side by side, his soft grey sweater around my shoulders, my head leaning against him. I think we look more like a couple of teenagers on a bench than the couple of teenagers on the bench opposite do.

Above us, the expansive inky sky is a canvas of star-shaped stars, their cut-out shapes something I've marvelled at since I first visited this country. I stretch my legs out straight, my bare feet through the grass, and I remember when we arrived here. Arrived to stay. Steve and I sitting quiet and close, like this, but on the sand, alone. The sun was so bright that day that its reflection made it hard to see if there was an ocean at all. But I knew there was. I could feel it loosening things. Preventing hard edges.

He kissed me when we got back that first evening, his hand on my knee, the ignition slowing in front of our new house, this house. And I had felt him like a want in me. We ran inside, down the empty hall, Steve lifting his shirt over his head and kicking his flip-flops out of the way as he ran, laughing.

We had left Dublin a week before, managing to outrun our past together. And we'd no reason to look in his rear-view mirror.

I straighten up now, begin to move. Everyone follows my lead – they start to gather knives and forks, glasses and bottles, napkins and ketchup, salad bowls smeared with oily bits of lettuce, all the detritus of the evening, from across the table. We carry it into the full light of our kitchen. Everything found and stacked for washing or put away. Nothing left behind.

'Time for bed, *mo stór*,' I say to Mae. She unfurls slowly, cushions moving, her little feet reaching to find the wooden floor of the porch.

'*Mo stór*. What does that mean?' Lisa asks.

'It means *my darling*.'

'*Mo stór*,' she says quietly to Al, and puts her hand on his, covering most of it, just his nails remaining exposed. Two lines of nails, hers painted black.

Mo stór.

Oíche mhaith. Good night.

I think I use these phrases more here. Or maybe I always did, but I'm just noticing it now. Perhaps I'm far enough away from Ireland to feel my affection for it.

Croí briste. Broken heart.

* * *

An earthquake ripped through the South Island a few weeks ago. We didn't feel it here in the north, but we could sense the upheaval in the news reports, the earth's release in the air. The land dealing with pressure. Adapting.

Nothing stays the same for too long. And I like that.

But, of course, this also means that nothing can last.

It was a small decision, nothing really, to have a second cup of tea after all – just half a cup – that morning, a week later, before I left for an early appointment at Mae's school. But it meant that I was still at the kitchen table when Steve came back from emptying our mailbox. And I was still there when he opened the pale blue envelope addressed to him in polite, cursive handwriting.

Had I been gone, I wouldn't have seen how he shrank back into the worktop. How he placed his left hand on it to support himself. How he seemed to be reading and rereading what looked to me like a very short letter, a single embossed page. How the page creased at its centre as he gripped it in his hand.

And the paperclip. I wouldn't have seen it fall to the floor when he pulled at something attached, at something smaller behind the page. A photo.

And the photo. I wouldn't have been there to see him, to see his face, to watch his eyes widen looking at that photo for the first of what would be many, many times.

'What is it?' My voice is even, despite the panic barely held back, waiting, waiting to rise through me.

'It's a photo of a child. A child. It's—' He looks stricken, holding the photo awkwardly, away from his face, from his body, as though it's a bomb he doesn't want to touch but is afraid of dropping. It quivers in his hand.

'It's what?'

'It says she's . . . eh, it says that . . . Oh, God. It says she's my child. I don't—' He stops.

Something punches through me.

She. My child.

'Show me.'

'I – I don't – I mean, it could be anybody. It's just a—'

'Steve. Show me. Please.'

'The letter's from that woman, you know, the woman from a few years ago. That time – back when we weren't getting on so well.' He turns the photo around.

It's a child. A girl. About three years old, maybe a bit more. A little girl, posing for the camera, holding out one side of a princess dress. He gives it to me and it quivers in my hand too. With thick, raven hair and dark eyes.

Al. She looks like Al. And Al looks like his father. The best of his father.

And some part of me knows immediately that it's true. Without hearing anything else, I believe it. My husband has a daughter. A second daughter.

And I can see that this comes as news to him too.

The room splits and tilts, everything in it seeming to swim away from the centre. I open the window above me for air, even though every glass door and wall in the kitchen is already pulled back, fully open, the room more outside than in.

'Beth, oh, God, Beth . . .' Steve reaches for me, and I lean into him. We stand there, staring at the photo, silence pounding through the room.

I turn it over. Her name – Olivia – is written on the back.

'Olivia,' he says.

A beautiful name. Ruined for me now. She is alone in the picture, but someone else's hand is visible. A hand holding one of hers. An adult's. But the adult has been cut from the photo with scissors.

Calculations and dates and years and ages. April 2013. I try to add, to count on. Born early in 2014. The months match. I know she is his. Somewhere deep down and instinctual, I know.

My husband has a second daughter.

A second chance for him.

A tornado builds around us, around the kitchen, readying itself to grab everything into its swirl and build, build, build, before firing it all to the ground and blowing out every glass window and door. Blowing out our very walls.

I want to get under the table to avoid it. To save myself and my clenched heart.

I hand the photo back to Steve, who casts about the

room for somewhere to put it. He sticks it on our fridge door. That's what we always do with new photos. Stick them on the fridge. We both stare at it in silence. He has used two magnets, even though one would have sufficed. A magnet at the top and another at the bottom. To cover more of it, I think, rather than to ensure it doesn't slide down.

It can't stay there, even with her face and legs hidden now as they are.

It's beside Mae's cardiac check-up appointment card and the phone number of a new speech therapist. They both have one magnet each.

It can't stay there. Hanging, weighing down a branch of our family's tree.

Al and Mae will see it. And Steve's father, Bill. And everyone else who comes through the door.

It can't stay there, dragging every eye towards it, sucking the air from the room. This photo of a little girl who is nearly four.

He passes me the letter. It is just one page and the writing is clear and neat, but the words jumble and jump off it. Snatches of sentences hitting home, slapping at me.

Dear Steve,

I hope you remember me . . . baby in January 2014 . . . New Zealand at the end of October . . . for six weeks . . . Olivia . . . back to London in December . . . meet you.

Jane

She was a January baby. Like Mae. But younger. Younger by four years. Another baby girl. But this one would have been perfect. She would have looked perfect. And they are coming here later this month to New Zealand. This woman and her child.

Here.

We have been found.

I don't say anything. Shock doesn't make a sound. Shock unleashes invisible waves that blow through a room and hollow out a person, a family. Shock presses against a person's temples and pushes, pushes, the pressure making them scrunch up their eyes to withstand it. Shock grabs at your throat so you can't breathe, and every breath becomes conscious, an effort. Shock makes your heart race. *DANGER, DANGER! Get out!*

I get out.

I sit on the wooden bench at the end of our street.

A perfect little girl. No therapies. No interventions. No surgeries on her broken heart. *Croí briste.*

I regret not taking the photo with me. I want to scrutinise it, to take in every tiny grain of this child, stare her away, stare her out of existence. My husband's child. I want to look at the photo until the shock of it wears off and she's been neutralised.

And, yet, I never ever want to see it again.

Her hair, her eyes, her skin. All her father's.

I wonder what else she has of his. What things she has been given, without our knowledge. His mannerisms, his head for numbers, his weaknesses? Acid sits in the back of my throat. Then again, maybe she has nothing of his. She has never been around him. Is it nature or nurture? She only has nature. But that seems a lot.

I feel a familiar desire, an old sense of wanting to go back to yesterday, to before I knew. The same feeling I had once before, when another little girl came into my life. After Mae was born and her disability declared, I wanted time to turn back then too. Back to before my world and everything in it slanted, lost its balance.

The photo. In its absence, I fixate on it.

Why send that photo? One that needed cutting. A photo that will be studied and remembered always, one that carries a life-changing message. A fucking bomb of a message from the other side of the world.

The photo was posed and its margins framed to include what had been decided upon. But, later, something was excluded. Someone. This photo, narrow and uneven down one side, more than a sliver of it having been cut away. Just a hint of someone left behind – a hand. Is it her mother's? A hand my husband knows.

Did Jane cut herself out of the photo at the last minute, after second and maybe third thoughts? Did she regret that decision after she posted it?

Or maybe the image wasn't posed at all. Maybe she just sent whatever photo she had lying around at the time – cut out a washing line or something ugly that sat to one side of it. No need to send her laundry to the other side of the world.

Now I regret not taking it with me because I want to rip it to shreds. I'm not sure if it'd be an act of healing or violence. Most likely a bit of both.

Of course, it's the letter I should have taken with me. I should have taken it, given myself time to organise the words into lines and the space to read between them.

Dear Steve

The intimacy of those two words, handwritten to my husband. Reminding him. Reminding me.

Strangers call him Steven. Not Steve.

I am trembling.

January 2014. Olivia would have been born while we were on holiday here, Steve and I, Al and Mae. My family. It would have been six months after the surgery that had repaired our daughter's stretched and heavy heart, when we came to see how life in New Zealand might be. During that trip we'd decided to give it a try, to move here.

January 2014. Jane would have been in London, thinking about my husband. She would have seen his colouring in her new baby. And she would have thought about him most days since. Olivia keeping Steve alive in her mother's mind. On the other side of the world.

And now Jane is coming. Here. With her daughter.

His daughter.

They are coming.

We have been found.

* * *

What is the term for children with the same father? Half-sisters – is that what they're called? A half-brother?

Jane can keep all of Olivia. We don't even want half of her.

* * *

Panic. My marriage. I want my husband like never before. I want to keep him from this woman. From this child. I want to ward them off. Panic. I imagine them ricocheting off us, off our house. Being fired into the air and far away.

What does she want, this woman? What does she want from us?

Panic.

And why now?

Does she want Steve? Did she want him four years ago, want him in her life? Is there more to their story than I know? More than I was told, after I asked, back then.

Back after the shock of our daughter's birth, after Down syndrome, after fear and sadness and confusion, a child for life. After Steve's weeks returned to their normality and importance, full of travel and promotion, nothing holding him back. After mine closed in, diminished, opportunities curdled and became buried, trivial, under the weight of having a disabled child. Of being a mother for life. Before I adjusted.

Back when I was lost and angry and hurt. When time passed and Steve still didn't want to get into it, didn't dare, and instead retreated and grew resentful. Back then.

Back when it was easier to live out our months with distance, together yet apart in our big, brash house, undressing with our backs to one another.

When Mae was three and life had been serious, lonely, for quite some time.

That's how we were, that's who we were, when I saw the hairbrush in his hotel room in April 2013. He'd Skyped the kids and me from one of his business trips to London. I couldn't hear him speak because all I could see was the glare of a cerise-pink hairbrush on the side-table behind him.

His cries when I confronted him. When he was home and I asked, when he was caught. Each breath and cry torn out of him. Caught. And how I hated him then, in that moment, everything about him – the back of his head, the curve of his shoulders – my heart thunderous in my ears while he apologised and pleaded, his arms out to hold me.

I remember my hot tears, my breaths coming in gulps and judders, as I drowned in my hate and my love for him.

We are a family. My husband and I and our two children. Nothing will change that, I tell myself now, over and over.

But – but another child to support financially, with everything that Mae requires. Will always require. This will change things. It will change everything.

And why now? Is this some kind of revenge on Jane's part? Revenge for Steve not being in touch, for leaving her alone? Because if it is, she is a woman serving her dish frozen solid.

* * *

It's late morning and Steve is in the garden with Mae. I know because I can hear their laughter through the open window above my side of the bed. He thinks he's letting me sleep on, but I've been awake most of the night. I felt him waken and get up earlier but kept my eyes closed until he had left the room.

I am lying still, rigid with despair. I've had a headache since Tuesday. Five days now. My body knows what's going on. It doesn't need documents or birth certificates or DNA tests. There's a tear now in the fabric of the life we've sewn ourselves into. A bloody big tear in our life together.

Jane and Olivia will be here in ten days' time.

And Steve's fucking birthday party is tonight.

* * *

Up the steps to our porch come the first of our guests. The rest will arrive steadily over the next half-hour, carrying bottles of wine, flowers, covered salad bowls, maybe even a plant pot with a short fern in it for me. And there will be cards and gifts for Steve.

This afternoon he cleared his throat a lot around me, but never got out the words that were stuck in it.

Everywhere our neighbours and friends are chatting, laughing, drinking, some talking over the music, others tapping along to it. They hold their glasses aloft, nodding at Steve as he passes through, beckoning him to come over. He smiles and raises his hand, keeps walking. He is busying himself, moving, moving, smiling and pointing ahead at somewhere outside or in the other room, somewhere he has to be, can't stop to talk just now.

'Can I get you another?' Does a few jokey dance steps on his way past. Laughter. 'I'll be right back.'

I see his father watching him with careful eyes, knowing something is wrong. Bill Rogers is eighty-eight and his legs no longer take his weight for long. Even so, he is still a fine man, a big man, with solid good looks. He's in a wheelchair a lot of the time, but it struggles to contain him.

I love Bill – he's been my living proof of good, honest men. He gave me something to believe in before I married his son, and every day since. He's always been a man of curiosity, but has had a few small strokes over the last year. Each time a tiny part of him is lost to us – a little corner of interest and wisdom hard won over the decades breaks off and falls away. Some days, he makes little impression in a conversation, but on his lucid days, when the fog lifts, he can be perceptive and whip-sharp. And he still knows his only son like the back of his hard-working hands.

Steve is standing alone out on the front porch, his back partially turned to me. I go and stand next to him, slipping my arm around his waist. I'm wearing a dress I know he likes, the red one he always remarks on. I see him looking at it, at me, as if I'm a stranger he can't quite recall meeting before. He rubs his forehead and yawns, a mannerism when he's uneasy. We think we know our partners, sometimes better than ourselves, and often we're right. We do, because we've studied them, watched them for years. We have heard how their voice changes under pressure. When they reveal themselves, our watchful eye catches it, catches them. The tic, the slip, the yawn. Steve mutters something about getting back in, about refilling drinks.

He moves away. I turn and watch him go, and see Bill has moved to the window and is looking out towards us.

I go out onto the front lawn, where the dark is absolute. The hum of conversation is quieter out here and it's the crickets I listen to. Simple, predictable night-time sounds. I look back at our house. Our rented house – a borrowed home – with its glass walls and doors. All the better to see you through, my dear. Looking in at our friends in the yellowed light, at the warmth and the goodwill, at our life here, I notice I've been living in a display case these past few years. I suppose it's easy to live in a glass box when you've nothing to hide, when your life is one worth showing, worth framing. And it has been.

Our friends in front of me now are characters lit on a bright stage, dancing, smiling, laughing, living the simple version of our story. The old version without the facts – without the *fact* of another child.

And I'm out in the darkness of the pit, already in the know, watching. I'm waiting until the discovery is made and the story takes a turn, until the curtains are pulled on us.

The photo. I think about it again, and the sheer weight of this – the shocking potential of my own thoughts –

physically pulls me down. I sit on the grass looking in, looking up at my life – the life I had until a week ago – longing for the wonderful ignorance of it.

Our home here, away from everything we knew. The old skin. But now it has found us, and is circling, shedding, snakelike.

And then I see Steve leave through our side gate and walk down the street, towards the harbour. A creature out after dark, sloping down the hill. Leaving his own party. I'll have to go back in. We can't both be gone. Someone must facilitate this evening, facilitate our lives.

Fragments of conversation reach me just for a moment so I know a door has opened and closed.

'Is everything okay, Beth?' Bill's gentle voice comes from the deck.

I look up at him.

'Some days start badly,' he says, 'and others end that way.'

'Yes, they do,' I say, and smile.

His own father had been a coarse, unfeeling man, and Bill had done everything to stop such traits in their tracks and not pass them down to his only son. He had been the opposite – kind, warm and attentive to his child. Even more so after his wife's death when Steve was just a teenager. And although their conversation, these days, is invariably about sport – the simplest currency between men of different ages – he and Steve adore each other, and their bond remains a deep and truthful one.

It doesn't seem right that I should be the person to tell him that his son has another daughter, that he himself has another granddaughter. This man, struggling to hold onto his mind, his understanding. I want to, because I need to tell someone and he's a good someone, but I imagine him leaning forward in his wheelchair the better to catch my words, to make sense of what I'm saying, to make sense of his son. While I'm sitting on the grass in the dark.

Maybe I can't say it out loud anyway. Maybe I don't want to let those boxed-up words out into the world to become real and run riot. Fire. Touching all that I know.

I turn away, look down the hill towards the water. I can't see it now. I know it's at the end of the road, silent and reassuring, but everything's too dark. Just the odd light here and there, marking out the top of the sailboats, wondrous little fireflies shining against the black.

The party goes well. Everybody says so. Steve and I smile as they leave, thank them for everything, but really for leaving.

In bed, he lies behind me, kisses my shoulder, the back of my neck, wrapping his body around mine in the silence. We are both quiet, afraid that words or tears might slip out if we don't stay on guard. So, silence instead.

What is it I would have him say?

We're both in the dark, knowing nothing yet.

* * *

When he comes through the door after work each evening, there are a few fraught moments when we see each other again, assess where we are, come down from the distance of the hours spent apart, wonder if the other has reached any conclusions.

Do you have a plan? Is there a magic wand?

I think of things to talk to him about, subjects that interest him, the ones that bind him to me and make us a unit: meeting his father for lunch; Al's university options; plans for that trip away; Mae's swimming without armbands. I want to catch his attention and hook it in, reel him towards me.

I hear him arriving home today. He pauses in the doorway before coming to stand by me at the kitchen counter. 'This won't change anything. It won't change us, Beth. I promise,' he says.

But I know, already I'm absolutely certain, that isn't true.

He goes to say something else, his mouth starts to make the shape, but then he decides against it. After a moment, he suggests ordering pizza for the kids.

* * *

The hours twist and turn onto themselves, dark to light and back again, the movement of soft clouds outside changing the light and the shadows on the walls inside our borrowed house.

I know I have to fully face this *news*, face myself.

Because there is a child involved. Not one child but two. Three, if you count Al, and I do.

Anxiety and fear and panic – all one and the same, really, interchangeable, whirling and dancing together, smiling, showing their teeth, felling as they go.

* * *

We go out for dinner. Just the two of us. To connect, to settle our boat.

I want to talk it out, talk and talk until the circle has decreased so much that only a manageable dot is left. But also I don't want to talk about it at all. Ever. Jane and Olivia. I don't want to bring them up, to make him think about them. Foolish of me. As though he isn't thinking about them every hour of the day. I don't know which of them threatens me more. As a pair, they're my tsunami.

Sitting opposite me, he says nothing. We are chess players, polite and restrained, waiting for the other to make a move.

I try to distract him, to distract myself. I ask if he fancies us taking his father's boat out on the water this weekend. He straightens up a bit at that. 'Maybe.'

He clears his throat then, and I think, *This is it – this is where the big conversation starts.* I ready myself, clasp my hands together and look him in the eye. My heart pounds.

'They're very slow,' is what he says. He looks around, then asks, 'Why are they so slow?' He motions at the various tables. 'It's not like it's even that busy. And there's certainly more than enough staff.' He stands up. 'We should leave,' he says. His chair pushes back with the movement. 'Don't you think we should leave?'

I don't move. He sits down again. Checks his watch. Looks at me.

We stay. We order and we wait. He won't enjoy being out, won't enjoy his meal. I know this before any food has come to the table. He needs to get back. Needs to get home and shut the door, close down the day. He wants to curl up with his anxiety and withdraw, the way he does when things are difficult.

But I need to stay out. At least out, we're together. In a way.

Steve looks about, checks his watch again, pointlessly. The waiter brings our food, and my husband sees there is nothing to be done now but eat it, or return untouched dishes and suffer a concerned interrogation from the staff, maybe a conversation about paying.

He is antsy; everything is too little, too much.

He eats quickly, as always. He's never refused anything put in front of him.

Then his plate is empty but I'm still moving my food around mine, creating small piles and spaces between.

As is his routine, he orders a rich dessert and coffee. He has made a kind of peace with seeing this out now, so he sticks to his ritual. But he won't enjoy it. He'll eat and drink every bit, but he'll be sure not to enjoy it. His mood, his balance, everything is off.

I try to play the supporting role of jocular woman to his burdened man. It gives me something to focus on. Being the agreeable foil. Even though my heart is sore and my stomach moves in waves, I smile and squeeze my husband's hand while we wait for the bill. He smiles at me, his expression broken and weary.

Everything is off.

* * *

Outside, everything goes on as normal.

I stand in the kitchen as the uncaring morning sun makes the usual patterns on the pavement. Shines on, regardless. I watch the way it moves in panels as cars pass and I hear the voice of a neighbour calling to someone, maybe to me, an arm waving in my direction. Just another ordinary day.

But inside, inside is a scream. Inside, it's not an ordinary day. Love and pain and fear are clanging off everything in this room, off each other, off shiny worktops and glass walls, and I want to slump to the floor to escape them. To put my shaking hands over my face and take cover.

But I don't.

I busy myself around the place. I am protecting what is mine. Who is mine. I smile. Keep it normal. Keep it in.

Everything is fine!

I become my mother.

Steve's impatient feet drum a steady rhythm back and

forth across the wooden floor. There are occasional pauses in the beat before it starts up again, back and forth, back and forth. Although my eyes are on the pot in the sink, my mind is across the room listening to his movements. By his patterns, you shall know him. I know him, all right, and I know how he is faring today. On this extraordinary day.

He looks tired. I know this too, even though he is behind me. Because he has looked tired for at least a week now. For eleven days, to be exact.

Ten nights have passed since we got that letter in the post, and I've stayed awake for most of them. Staring at the ceiling and thinking about this girl. I never get up, though. I stay there, beside my husband. So I can be near him, can see him there, just lying.

Lying.

I went to him when I heard him come through the door yesterday. I put my arms around his neck, I smiled – to keep him, to keep our love, to hold the basic things between us, to feel his body against mine. Mine.

I touched his shoulder in bed, gently.

Hello?

He responded. And it was us, there under the rubble. Something vital and real.

But we didn't talk afterwards.

I remember Steve saying something to me once, at a party a long time ago, when we bumped into an old boyfriend of mine: 'At any one time, I want to be the only man in the room to have slept with you. So let's go.' And I remember how sexy it was then, as we left together, hand in hand, our smiles full of fire and promise. There'd be nothing sexy about it if I said it to Steve now. Shortly. When Jane's in our kitchen. *At any one time, I want to be the only woman in the room to have slept with you. So she has to go.*

No one would be fucking smiling then.

And then the suddenness of her, here in the room.

'Jane.' A hand is extended in front of me. Her first word her own name.

And although I've known that she was coming for days now, there is something extraordinary about Jane appearing here. Bang! And she is in this house. Transported. So far from where she belongs. Something magical about it. No, not that. Something unreal. Macabre.

Her blonde hair falls in straight sheets with a blunt, heavy fringe. Her face in a frame. She tilts her head, taking me in, even though surely it's her who should be under scrutiny.

I take the hand but can't reply.

'It's a pleasure, Beth,' she says then.

My name in that mouth. Only four words, but enough for me to hear a refined English accent. And I'm certain there is little pleasure in this for either of us.

She is tall. Much taller than me. Nearer to Steve's height. I'm wondering how he could have gone for someone so tall. But maybe he hadn't noticed. When they met, they were sitting down, or so the story goes. But they must have stood up to go to the lift and to—

I breathe in, give her a slight nod. I'm standing close enough to kiss her on both cheeks if I were French and less hung-up, better able to shrug off all of this liberal carry-on. *Le sex? Avec mon homme? C'est rien!*

I'm also close enough to slap her.

I can't bear them to shake hands – her and Steve – I can't bear that they will touch. Will he kiss her cheek? This woman who made him forget his marriage?

He steps forward. 'Hello,' in an outdoor boom.

She walks to him, her high heels tap-tap-tapping are elegant ice-picks stabbing our floor. He shakes her hand firmly, sawing up and down, business-like. No nonsense to see here.

'Hi,' her sultry quiet response. *Smile.*

I imagine taking her shoes off and killing her with them.

Haven't you touched each other enough? I want to shout.

I allow my eyes to flicker over her. She is slim, dressy in a sophisticated, made-an-effort way. More glamorously turned out than I would be in the circumstances, I think. But, then, there's no dress code for this.

What was the connection they had? Do they still have it? What had been the attraction? Is it still there? Is there electricity here now? I can only feel nausea.

I look to Steve and think I see his eyes slide down her hair, and I remember – a blinding flash – the hairbrush on the bedside locker in his hotel room that morning. The shape, the curve, the glaring cerise-pink shock of it. Searing. I see it clearly now, despite the intervening years of love and sunshine baking a hearty family crust over it.

The Skype call he made to re-set his life, re-set his sense of himself after his night with her.

They look one another over, and my underarms prickle with a hot pain. I want to crawl out of my skin, being present for this reunion. My mind shuttles through stills from that night, and I wasn't even there. I assume their minds do too, and now the jumble of those heated moments from the past is spilling all over our beautiful, light-filled home here at the end of the earth.

What are they remembering?

Opening each other's buttons in the lift.

Their images would be better than mine – more detail, lurid. Real.

Their kiss sliding them across a wall in the long hotel corridor, him carrying her, her legs around him, trying to find the right room, the plastic card into the slot, bumping through the door, falling, laughing, teeth against teeth.

Do they both recall it in the same way? No. Foolish to think that. Men only remember the main event.

Does she remember romance and feelings of fate? Is that what's brought her here? Notions about the one who got away. She looks young enough for that to be possible.

Words and questions and screams clatter through my mind, and my chest feels stood on, my skin itchy and alive.

I move to stand next to my husband. 'We've been expecting you,' I say ridiculously.

That smile again.

And now I'm wondering if she left the brush on purpose. I am experiencing her, everything about her, for the first time. We never look at someone as powerfully as we do the very first time. Jane.

But Steve has an edge on me, even now. He's seeing her *again*. Is she living up to his first impression of her? His last impression of her? Is he seeing her as more, or as less? Of course Jane is more to him now, no matter how she looks. She is his daughter's mother. Like I am. She will always now be more than before.

'How have you been?' she asks him.

My breath catches. *How have you been?* As though she had ever known how he was in the first place. *How have you fucking been?* Reminding me that they have *known* each other. Reminding him of confidences shared.

I want to step between them, divide them. I want to put my hands over his eyes so he can't see her. And yet I can't look away from any of it. I have a perverse desire to injure myself by soaking up every second of this brutal farce. How much can I take?

'Steve told me all about – about meeting you. At the time,' I say. It's important to me that I get this in quickly. Important to me that she knows, although he is a cheat, our marriage is so wonderfully strong that he was able to be honest about being a cheat. That we had quite the chat about it. 'Back when it happened,' I go on. 'He told me everything.' I wince through the last word, hearing myself. Of course he didn't tell me *everything*. He didn't walk me through the evening's highs and lows. Or those of the following morning. And she knows it. We all do.

She nods, and I can't tell if she's amused or embarrassed. I know without looking that Steve is mortified, but he doesn't move and he doesn't speak. And I don't want him to, because then she would have reason to turn to him, to look at his face. And he could do the same. So I talk endlessly, haul my attention to normal, mundane topics to force her to engage with my conversation. I need them both to keep their eyes on me so that they can't rest them on each other. I am taking control of things between us, even though obviously that horse well and truly bolted years ago and I wasn't even told that there were races.

I talk about this neighbourhood. I ask about her journey here – like I give a shit. I steer our chat, and all the while my pulse is booming in my neck. I can hear my rushed words, all of me running to catch my breath and keep going. Just keep going. My words judder along, the emphasis in all the wrong places.

When my manic sentences have run on and on and finally out, Steve takes over but his voice is strangled. Where my words were tumbling and racing, his are cagey and suspicious. Anything you say may be held against you.

He is walking through broken glass, where I was firing bottles against the walls. His face is red, the way it gets when his blood pressure rises. While he cautions his way through careful words and sentences, she and I nod at intervals.

Pressure building everywhere but nobody prepared to take a pin to it.

Then Jane smiles, and my thoughts fill with the bad theatre of hotel sex, all arched backs and tossed hair, sultry smiles and noisy sighs, where everything is new and has been waxed and tanned and painted, ready for display – lights, sheets, action. Not the darkness and duvets of years.

I'm boiling the kettle again when I hear her laugh at something he says. Laughter! Here, in this cauldron of a room. There will be no humour. I spin round to see what could possibly cause one to laugh during a nightmare such as this. But there is nothing to see, no slapstick, no clown. No room in the laugh for me.

I wonder if it's a private joke, something remembered, something shared. My mind turns on itself, imagining this joke the first time round, tangled bed linen, laughter.

Am I the joke?

Jane's gone. Our normal speech patterns and some level of survivable pressure are beginning to return to the kitchen. Steve looks less like he's having a panic attack and more like his actual self. And then I think that maybe she was just nervous and laughing at nothing because, after all, she doesn't know anything about us. She doesn't know him. Not really.

We've arranged to meet here again in a couple of days' time. I hope she looks worse then, even though I know the opposite will be true because Olivia will be with her.

* * *

'She isn't four yet. So everyone will know. The Rogers family – you, your son aged nineteen, your daughter aged seven, your daughter aged three, and your wife of twenty years,' I hiss, torturing us both. My words swipe, slice through our bedroom.

'Stop, Beth. Please.' Steve's voice is low. 'I know, honey. I don't know what you want me to . . .' His words trail off and he presses hard on his eyes with his hands.

I can't remember the last time I cared what people thought. But I do now. About this. Because it means I will have to explain it. I will have to explain her. And I will have to explain my flimsy fucking husband.

* * *

'She is as blonde and as slim as I feared,' I tell Claire. 'And younger than me, of course.'

'How much younger?'

'Fifteen years or so, I'd say. Probably in her early thirties.'

'Jesus. That's annoying in itself.'

'She probably grew up with the internet.'

'And she really is blonde?'

'As blonde as clichés would have you believe. That's exactly what she is.'

Claire shudders. 'Has she other kids?'

'No.'

'Has she met his? Yours, I mean.'

'Not yet.'

'But she knows about them?'

'She knows he has two. I don't know what else she's been told. I don't know anything, really. Why the fuck is that?'

Claire and I sit silently and wonder what Jane mightn't know about Mae.

'I catch myself imagining him with her back then, putting his hand on her thigh as they sat on bar stools. Is that mad?'

'No. It'd probably be weird if you didn't.'

'Yeah, but I have almost an adolescent level of hyper-sensitivity towards her. When she was there, I was all eye-rolls and sighs. Any maturity I had seemed to desert me. She swanned through the room scattering stardust, and I just wanted to club her over the head.'

Who made the first move? That's what I don't know. And for some reason it seems important now. Like it would tell me something about her. Or confirm something I might suspect about him. I don't say it, though. Not to Claire, not to anyone.

'She has some balls showing up here,' she says. 'On the other side of the world! I think we can assume she isn't here to play the struggling victim.'

'She says she just wants Olivia to know him. Her *father.*'

'I suppose I can credit that,' Claire says.

I puff out my cheeks, exhale.

'Is the kid's photo still stuck up in your kitchen?'

'No. Although if it was, it would stop me ever going near the fridge again. And then I'd be skinny. Which would at least be something.'

'True. You still wouldn't be as young as her mother though.'

* * *

Did he tuck her long hair behind her ears to hold her face before he kissed her?

His fingers on her skin.

We all want something beautiful, as the song goes.

But it's in the past.

And it shouldn't happen again.

* * *

Without warning, I'm crying. When I realise it, when I identify the cold itch on my cheeks as tears, I'm surprised. I have become a woman who sits and weeps alone in public. I feel disconnected from everything in that moment, from myself.

I should walk back to my car, get in, compose myself. But I don't think I can. I don't think I feel up to it. And I don't care to try.

* * *

I saw a nail file poking out of her bag and imagined her sharpening her nails into points with it.

* * *

The horror washes over Al, his face and body wavering, disbelieving everything his father – his beloved father – is telling him. He looks at me to refute what he's hearing, to bring some common sense, to steady his world. A second opinion.

This is a joke, right?

He gives the photo the smallest of glances. 'She looks like me,' he says. 'She looks more like me than my actual sister does.'

He hands the photo back to Steve and leaves, the screen door slamming in his wake.

* * *

'So tell me what she's like, this woman?'

My mother flattens her skirt across her knees with both hands in a gesture of readiness. She sits still today, giving my drama her full attention.

'Well, obviously I don't really know her, but she's tall and seems quite self-assured.'

'Oh, yes.' My mother already knows her very well indeed.

'Confident, I suppose I'd say—'

'Full of herself, you mean, Beth,' she cuts in, having heard enough. She leans forward, her face looming large on the screen. Her highlighted hair is lacquered into waves and moves as a set piece while she nods. 'I know the type exactly. Used to smiling at all the right people – all the right *men*. And the wrong ones, too, no doubt.' She tuts loudly. 'Oh, but, my darling, she's no match for you.'

And, actually, I'm glad I called her.

* * *

'I've thought about this moment so many times over the last few days.' Steve is speaking to me but I'm distracting myself by looking at Al's paintings hanging in our lounge. One painting in particular: layers and layers of brushstrokes and dark patterns building up to resemble a distressed wall. 'I've thought about little else, really. What will it be like?' he goes on, wondering aloud. 'The magic or the disaster of it. I've imagined every eventuality at this stage, and I'm no more prepared. I don't feel I'm ready at all. I still can't picture it, Beth. It just doesn't seem real.'

Olivia is due here now with her mother and I'm staring at walls, wishing I'd painted more, that I'd kept it up. I remember how calming it was. The process, the achievement. I'm forcing my mind to stay on painting, but Steve keeps talking.

'I want it to go well, but then I think of you and Mae and Al, and think that maybe it would be better if it didn't. Didn't go well. You know?'

Yes, I do.

'If it all fell apart and no more came of it.'

Yes, please.

'But that's not really what I want. I mean, I do want to meet her. I have to. To see her. You know? To see this child with my own eyes. And I'd like if it went at least not disastrously.'

I speak now, because I know he'll keep talking until I do. Until I reassure him, until he hears something he can interpret as positivity. 'I don't know how it will play out, Steve, but I'm pretty sure you'll take to her and she to you, more than you think.'

That's the truth. And that's why I feel so sick about it.

I know he'll have pictured her tiny hand reaching for his because he enjoys the idea of being a hero.

'I feel like I'm preparing for an exam,' he says.

I take a chocolate lollipop from my bag and hand it to him. His eyes fill and he touches my cheek. For a moment, I think he doesn't understand it's meant for Olivia.

'Here she is!' He jumps to his feet, his voice a bizarre wobbly roar.

I turn. And there she is, a child being led up the garden path.

The reality of her knocks the wind out of me. Her thick black hair, longer than in the photo, has been pulled into two perfect plaits.

And then she is in front of me. In front of us. Right here. Dark pools for eyes, framed by long eyelashes. She looks like my Al, and my chest hurts when I see it, the force of the resemblance up close, alive.

Exhibit A. Living and breathing. Her father's daughter.

I'm not sure how to greet her so I bend down a little and shake her hand, just for a second. My husband's child's hand. My stomach is queasy with something that feels like sadness, only much worse.

We stand there, three adults, looking at her. Saying nothing. Staring at the child in the centre of the room. Appraising her. She has burst through an old door, one long since boarded up by Steve and me. And now she is the puppet master, our strings tangled around her small, clammy hands.

'Hello, Olivia.' I am the first to speak.

'Nice to meet you.' Her speech is clear.

She is about the same height as Mae, but younger. Slimmer, more delicate.

I wonder if Steve can see her familiarity, her strangeness. Or is he already a father? Everything about his child simply a wonder, no matter what.

I look at his face and it's the face of a man seeing a ghost. Even a move to the other side of the world won't outsmart the past, won't lay it to rest. One day it will find you, ring your doorbell, and come into your home with a an English accent and plaits in its hair.

He hasn't made a sound. Jane stands back, waiting for something. Waiting to be addressed. She can wait.

'That's me.' Olivia is the one to break the silence. She's pointing at the photo on the fridge, put back there this morning. Temporarily.

'She looks like you.' Jane speaks now, presumably to Steve. She turns to me. 'Don't you think, Beth?'

'I suppose a little,' I say. She couldn't look more like him.

'Well, my family are all fair so she definitely gets her colouring from the Rogers side.' Jane fingers her daughter's dark plaits as she speaks.

I feel a stab of jealousy, but remind myself that Bill Rogers adores Al and Mae, and that if it ever becomes a question of sides, I know which one he'll be on.

I see confusion in Steve's face and sense hesitation in him. He has moved nearer to me. I touch his arm and nod.

He clears his throat. 'Hello there.' His voice is tentative, almost a whisper. 'It's lovely to meet you.' He puts his hand out to Olivia. A moment passes, and then she steps forward and shakes it quickly. 'What an adventure you're on,' he says.

Olivia looks at her mother.

'Coming all this way!' His words a little louder. 'And on such a big bus.'

'Not a bus!' She is suddenly animated and looking straight at him. 'A big plane, silly.'

'A big plane! Wow!' He smiles, he's getting going.

'That's pretty exciting. To travel so far, especially when you're so young.'

'I'm three and three-quarters.'

We know.

He hunkers down, looks into her face. Looking for himself.

She looks back, a mirror. Does she see herself in his eyes, in his colouring?

Children don't, though, do they? Not until they're older, if at all.

'Well, Olivia,' he says now, 'I'm very glad you've come here.'

These words, said so kindly to her, echo and scrape inside me. I imagine I see stitches form between the two of them, slowly pulling them together, knitting her into the fabric of his heart.

Olivia watches us over her shoulder as she leaves, and her mother tugs at her hand to get her to turn away. Important not to be rude. Important to have manners when you've just thrown a grenade at a family.

I want to put my arms around Steve to comfort him. But I also want him to look to me, to comfort me. My heart is open and reaching for him.

Jane gives him the briefest backward glance as she gets into her car. She is beautiful. I can't deny that. I look from her face to him, and it's the dark, brooding version I see beside me. Standing, staring after the car.

He is good-looking too. Maybe I should have worried more about that. About the choices it must have presented him with over the years.

I wonder if maybe *he* is the prize. If Jane is here for him, to claim him for herself. She could have her pick of men. But only one in the world is her daughter's father. And I know how alluring that is.

'You did well with Olivia,' I say. 'She liked you.'

He turns his head towards the sound and sees me, his face blank. Like he's just remembered I'm there.

I don't say anything else. It's not the time for small talk.

* * *

Fitful dreams disturb me that night. I see Olivia as a young boy and I waken wondering if that would be better for Mae.

But maybe it would be worse for Al.

Al. Will he see himself in Olivia when he meets her? Maybe he'll grow to love her. Could I bear it if he did?

Will all of this go over Mae's head? I hope so.

I turn to look at Steve beside me and see he is awake, staring at the ceiling, both of us keeping our thoughts inside.

* * *

I think about her all the next day, while I'm sitting in traffic, queuing at the supermarket. Olivia. Who knows what she must think of all of this, of being here? Probably nothing. Will she remember when she's older? Will she recall meeting her father for the first time? She might, because she was on holiday at the time. She'll probably remember ice cream and the beach.

But she is the reason her mother and father will always remember meeting for the first time.

Will Steve want to be there to enjoy the milestones in her life – her graduation, maybe a wedding, her children? The normal stuff. The stuff we've spent seven years convincing ourselves doesn't matter.

Steve turns from the TV when I come in. His face is puffy and his hair dishevelled. He closes his eyes in defeat and puts out his hands for me to go to him. I cross the room and stand next to him. He circles his arms around the back of my legs and hugs them – hugs me – to him. 'Sorry,' he says.

I put my hands over his. 'It's okay.'

* * *

'You can't just let her rock up here and turn our whole family upside-down.' Al paces the kitchen. 'Seriously, Mum. Are you just going to let this happen?'

'I don't want to, darling – believe me. But unfortunately I can't deny reality. Even though I wish with every cell of my being that I could. It is a reality. Olivia is your father's child.' The words sit like lead in my stomach, in my mouth.

My son's hands ball into fists at his sides. He is

outraged, with the noble and romantic passion of youth. He's at an age that deals only in absolutes. To him, being unfaithful is the worst thing in the world. A mockery of everything.

'We have to try to get our heads around it,' I say. 'And we have to love—'

'I WILL NOT BE LOVING HER.' His voice is loud and definite.

'I was going to say *him*. Your dad. Al, we have to love *him* through this, as we always have and will. It's Dad, honey. He's still the same man.'

'Not to me he isn't. I don't know who he is. He's a total idiot.'

'I understand you thinking like that. I did, too, for a while. But people make mistakes. Life can be difficult and good people – loving, kind people – make bad choices and do stupid things.'

I wish I could be as certain as my tone and words suggest. But as Al is still quiet, still here, I continue: 'I knew about his . . . his meeting this woman. He told me at the time.' I bend the truth in Steve's favour, as though he'd come clean when it happened, rather than after he'd been caught. I don't mention Steve's face, tear-streaked and ashamed, his eyes closed, as if he was in a confessional, when he told me about the bar in the airport hotel, his conversation with Jane, their chat about work, about their lives. I don't mention how I made him tell me all of it. How he'd said he hadn't taken her number or given her his, how flattered he'd said he felt, and then how stupid and heartbroken afterwards. I don't tell him how his father had wanted to put down the responsibility of us all just for a little while, or how deadened he'd felt after he did.

And I don't tell my son how I told Steve he had to go, before he and Mae got back that day. How defeated he had looked as he nodded. How I watched him pull shirts and trousers out of our wardrobe in Dublin, piling them into his suitcase – the very one I had packed for him earlier the same week for that trip to London – how I watched him pat the clothes down, pat the creases in with the flat of his hands. How I didn't help, how I didn't suggest that he should bring other shoes, or that he should remember to take underwear.

And I don't tell Al how I cried seeing his father's ashen face as he left, his jacket held in a ball against his chest, his walking out of the room dragging the pathetic little case.

And I don't tell him how I curled into myself on the bed, feeling I would never rise again.

I don't tell Al any of that.

I give a shake, shake the memory of that day back down inside me.

'And we dealt with it,' I say, 'and even though it was difficult for a while, we moved on from it and we were happy again. And life with you and Mae, our family, was good. Great, really. Everything ticked along.'

'Like a bomb.'

'I know it's a lot to take in, Al.' I put my hand on his. 'And I never imagined that there might be a child. It's come as such a huge shock, to be confronted with this, years later. But I still love your father, and he absolutely still loves us. Still loves you. Still loves Mae. Very much.'

He moves his hand so that I will take mine back.

'How can you stand it, though? How? Dad had sex with someone else and has a daughter to prove it.' He bangs his hand on the worktop. 'Another child. And you're defending him. Jesus, Mum.' He paces again. 'Dad. My dad. I mean, who is he? The man I know would never have cheated on us.'

* * *

'So was it a meeting of minds, then?' Claire asks me.

'Who? Jane and me, or Steve and Jane?'

'Steve and Jane.'

'I hope not. She's a total moron.' This isn't true. I can tell she's bright, ambitious. And if the judgement is based upon who's in control of the situation, who's belted into the driver's seat, then she's a whole lot brighter than Steve and I put together. 'I think she's probably quite adept at playing men, at being what they want. I spent the entire time feeling she was talking down to me, as though she had one over on me, you know – the old wife, the rickety marriage. That kind of thing.'

'And what was Steve doing during all of this?'

'Sitting there. Sweating. Panicking. My tea was almost cold by the time I could persuade my hand to pick it up without shaking. Or without throwing it over her.'

Claire laughs.

'The thing is – and I know this is ridiculous – I can't help feeling that if she fell for him before, then she must be bloody beside herself about him now. You know? He still looks good, fitter and tanned and all that, and now he's also her daughter's father.' I groan and put my head into my hands.

'Beth, I really don't think she came this far to check out his abs. Steve is not that hot.' She smiles.

'I know – and it's crazy but I just can't bear the idea of them *fancying* each other.' It sounds even more stupid aloud.

'To be honest, I'd say she's sorry she ever clapped eyes on him, and I don't imagine she'll be entertaining any thoughts of him in that way. This is purely about their, sorry, her daughter. I'd be sure of it.'

'But even just *that* is still *an awful lot.*'

* * *

'Why did she come, Steve? Why now?'

He looks at me over the newspaper. 'I don't know too many of the specifics as yet but I suppose she must feel it's the right time. She must have her reasons.'

'I know she must. Of course she does. This is a huge

trip to undertake with a child, even in more *normal* circumstances. So what are they? What are her reasons for coming this far, and for doing it now?'

What does she actually fucking want?

He folds the paper, places it on the table. 'I don't know. And I feel a bit pissed off that she waited this long, actually. That she didn't find a way to tell me she was pregnant, or that I had a daughter all this time. But, then, all the upset and the stress of it, you know? Maybe there's no good time for things like this. I suppose I should try to be glad that she contacted me at all, even four years later. But, honey, I don't know what her reasons are yet. I would tell you if I did.'

I breathe in. 'Are *you* one of them?'

'What? Well, yes, obviously. I imagine I'm the main one, really. Don't you?'

'I mean, *you*. Is it you she's after?'

'I am her child's father. And that's why she's here, so, yes, I suppose.' His face pleads confusion: he's still reluctant to go where I have.

I raise my eyebrows at him, then turn away, start wiping down the worktop surfaces, tidying at nothing.

'Beth, I'm the reason she's here in so far as I am – well, she *says* I am – Olivia's father. She's not here for *me*. As a man, or anything. If that's what you're asking.'

I don't reply but bend to start emptying the dishwasher. He chooses to interpret this as meaning that I'm satisfied, my query dealt with and filed.

'I love that I'm getting the opportunity to know them,'

he says then. 'To know her. Olivia.' He is standing beside me now, looking out the window. I continue putting our clean dishes away. 'To spend a little bit of time with her, you know. And I appreciate it, Beth, I really do, that you're supporting me in it.'

His tone is light: he has a growing ease with his comely version of events.

Knives, plates, glasses, all hot and glinting.

'She's a really lovely kid, I think,' he says, still looking out the window. 'Don't you?'

Who? Jane? I want to answer. But I don't need to say anything, because he speaks again.

'And I know the circumstances couldn't be any worse but she's just a little girl, and you can understand. Can't you? Understand how I must feel connected to her?'

I straighten, two forks in my hand.

'I'll finish that. You sit down,' he says, as I come closer to his level. He smiles at his own considerate loveliness.

There's just one spoon left to put away.

I look straight at him, but he misreads it and starts to hum cheerfully.

Sitting on the couch watching television later that evening, Steve rests his hand on my leg and my eyes fill with tears. Worn out as I am, the simple familiarity of this gesture in our lamp-lit room is at once just enough and also more than I can bear. A tiny grounding normality in a hurricane.

* * *

I'm thinking about Jane even though I'm not yet fully awake.

For a while, I'd managed to outrun my old self here in this new life. But now I've another woman to outrun. A younger one at that.

Or maybe it's our marriage that's catching me. The papered-over cracks finally peeling apart, rising up at their edges.

I squeeze my eyes tighter shut, try to remember some meditative mental exercises to calm and focus my mind. It focuses itself on who I would fuck if I got to take a night off from being married and was given the key to a hotel room. My heart is beating even faster now – I get up. I make the bed and fluff the pillows. I think about jumping on it, messing it up, but I don't. It'd be left to me to make it nice again.

* * *

I line my flip-flops up neatly next to Steve's on our front porch so that he might notice how small they are next to his. He's always liked how small I am, when I'm beside him. I suppose it makes him feel big.

How long have I been his fool?

No fool like an old fool, I remember my mother saying about my father. But only ever loud enough for me to hear.

* * *

Jane didn't know much about Mae. It's written all over her face.

Down syndrome pirouettes across the room.

'This is for you, Mae,' she says, speaking as though for the deaf. In her arms is a giant make-up set in pink and black packaging. Rows of sparkling eye-shadows, glossy lipsticks, finicky brushes and palettes of pressed powder and bronzers.

'Wow! Thank you! For my dolls?'

'Um, yes, I suppose. Yes, you could use it for your dolls. Or for you? Maybe? For your face.' Jane looks at me. 'Whatever you think, Beth. Would it be okay? On her . . .' She motions towards her own face, which has reddened.

Mae's disability is giving rise to a kind of simmering havoc in Jane, to which my daughter is oblivious.

'Mum! Look! Face paint!'

A child with Down syndrome.

It's heavy stuff, as the doctor told me when Mae was just a day old.

Hey, Jane. He has a child with Down syndrome. How d'ya like him now?

I'm standing here, hoping that my beautiful daughter will put a woman off my husband. That his disloyalty will be uglier now. That her disability will be my winning hand. I am disgusted with myself. But I can't say I'm not still hopeful.

Maybe we could get a paternity test for Olivia the next time we take Mae for her thyroid-function bloods.

Oh, the things I could say, now that I'm wicked and losing my grip.

'Mae. That's a lovely easy name to pronounce,' Jane's voice ventures, quieter than I've heard it before. 'Mae. Is that why you chose it for her?'

'It's actually Ismae. And, no, that's not why. Thank you for your gift, though.'

* * *

'You remember Julie Brooks?'

'I think, maybe . . .'

'You *do*, Beth. And her daughter Miranda? The youngest girl. Well, I ran into her today – Miranda, I mean, not Julie – and can you believe this? After all the trouble they had with her, everything she put them through, she ended up with an accountant. Miranda Brooks. Looking fabulous and ending up with an accountant!' My mother's face on my screen, her lipstick freshly applied.

What does that even mean? She 'ended up with'. Are they both terminally ill? On their deathbeds? Or does it just mean that they're married? Have a child? At any moment, it might all collapse. Be over in an instant. Next month might arrive with an explosive strapped to it and everything be levelled in minutes. Unless you are actually dead, you can't be said to have ended up with anything or anybody, surely.

My mother has probably been telling people for years that her daughter ended up with a New Zealander.

'Beth? Beth! For Heaven's sake! Are you even listening to me?'

She's there, watching.

'Sorry, Mum, I was miles away.'

'Well, that's certainly true. Honestly! At least your father has the courtesy to be in the same country when he's ignoring me.'

* * *

'I used to trust things. Well, mostly.' Al's voice is unsteady. He's twisting the string of his hoodie round and round and round. 'I mean, I know I've always been kind of serious and a bit of an over-thinker, but I did actually assume that the world could be trusted, you know, for the most part. That the adults knew what they were doing.' He stops and I wait. Wait for the difficult words to find the surface and make their way out. 'Dad. That Dad knew what he was doing, knew what mattered. That he was Safe Hands.' He snorts. 'All this time I've been leaning my ladder against the wrong wall, Mum.'

I put my arm around his shoulders, but say nothing. He wants only to be heard.

'I don't feel like I can trust anything now. The world itself, the people in it, everyone's just grappling around. Trying to make out what's real. And what's only a shadow. We're all just covering our tracks and hoping for the best. When there is no fucking best.'

He doesn't apologise for, or seem to notice, his language. And I don't react to it. It is, after all, appropriate.

* * *

It's three a.m., and I'm outside on our swing eating dry toast and considering the stars. Wondering at their twinkling, their power, their universal sway. Wondering what they already know, being light years ahead of us. I want to tune into their knowledge, to cut a deal, between bites.

Maybe their twinkling is laughter.

* * *

'I was thinking of planning a day out this week, of maybe taking the girls to—'

'The girls?'

'Mae and Olivia.'

'*Your* girls, then. Not *the* girls. I only have one,' I say.

He ignores my nonsense and continues: 'What do you think? So they can meet each other. And Jane could come. And you, of course. I'd like you to come too.'

I don't say anything.

'I was thinking maybe the zoo.'

'The zoo? We've never even been to the zoo here ourselves. I hate zoos. I thought you did too. All the confinement and queues and— What's wrong with the cinema, or something a bit easier?'

72

'You mean something a bit shorter.'

'That too.'

'Come on, honey. The zoo is outdoors, it's casual, we'll have space to chat, to move around. That kind of thing. The kids can have a bit of freedom. Whereas all of us in a row in the dark? The cinema isn't going to be much use to us getting to know her.'

'Getting to know who?'

'Olivia! Jesus. What is wrong with you?'

'I thought you meant her mother. Anyway, I'd rather see animals in their natural habitat.'

'Yes, thank you for that, Beth. I think most people would. But I don't think either of us wants to take Olivia and her mother—'

'Jane.'

'Yes, Jane,' he spoke slowly, clearly addressing an idiot, 'on fucking safari with us, so all in all, I think the zoo might be a better option.'

I look away. Four more weeks, that's all. Just four more weeks of them. Breathe.

He changes his approach. 'Beth, I know this is all very difficult and that it's revisiting something painful, I get that, but we need to get a handle on the situation and try to come to terms with it.'

'I don't want to go.'

'Okay.' He drums his fingers on the table, thinking on his feet. 'Yep. Okay, I can understand that.' He is a man at a work, chairing a meeting, brainstorming. Drumming his fingers, tapping out solutions. 'Mae might like you to be there and I'd rather we faced this, grasped it, together. But' – he's reasonable, he can work with a difficult client – 'I don't want to put you under any further pressure. So I'll do it myself. I'll take the girls and—'

'Again with "the girls". "I'll take the girls." Oh, fuck off, Steve. A one-night stand in a Holiday Inn years ago and now you're all about *the girls*. Why don't you just take a day off from being such a bloody great guy?'

He doesn't react badly to this but rather kneels in front of me and speaks quietly, patiently. Which is when I realise just how much he intends to win this one. He shall go to the zoo.

'I didn't mean anything by that, Beth. I just meant that I understand if you don't want to come.' Another deep breath. Tactical change. 'Okay, so what would you like to do?'

'I would like to go back to when this child didn't exist. Or even to the time when we didn't know that she existed. That would do.'

He moves my hair from where it has fallen to one side of my forehead and loops it behind my ear. 'They're here for six weeks, Beth. Just six weeks. Even less now – a little more than four. And I need to do what I can, to be part of it, for this very short time. Okay? Can you see that?'

I stare at the floor.

'Look, honey, you forget about the trip. The day out. The zoo. It's all too much. You plan a day for yourself, and I'll take Mae and Olivia,' he says their names slowly, separately, 'by myself. I imagine Jane might want to be there, too, but you don't—'

'Not a fucking chance. I'm coming.' I stand up and walk out of the room as though getting my keys to leave right that minute. I am barefoot and ridiculous, immediately zoo-ready and willing.

The art of the deal. Nicely played, Mr Rogers.

* * *

'What?' I stop brushing my hair and look at Steve.

He says nothing but makes a show of staring at his watch face before leaving our bedroom doorway.

'Jesus Christ! I'll be ready in a minute,' I shout after him.

I have dressed carefully. And I have dressed Mae twice. First, too well. We have nothing to prove. Second, too casually. She's not about to fingerpaint. But I leave it. I need to prove that we have nothing to prove.

Unfortunately, nobody has cancelled or thought better of it, so the three of us get into the car bound for the zoo.

I've always found Steve attractive behind the wheel, his ease of manoeuvre, the way his hand rests confidently on the wheel. But today I put sunglasses on and look out the window at my side. There's more to being a good man than mastering a three-point turn.

He and I don't talk to each other on the journey. Instead I chat to Mae, who is sitting behind me.

'You okay, Mama?'

I stretch my palm out, a starfish, and look at my nails as I answer her. 'Yes, darling. I'm okay.' I reach back and hold her hand for a moment. Reassurance. For me.

Steve goes to speak a couple of times as we near the zoo, but the first time I turn on the radio and the second time I increase the volume, so he ends up saying nothing.

I clasp my hands on my lap. Nun-like. Judgement dripping from me. Hating myself for it, but hating him more.

He stands at the entrance, looking this way and that. Jangling his keys. Checking his phone. Actively waiting. I counter by looking disinterested.

Mae is standing uncertainly. One parent pacing, the other sulking. Divining the tensions and invisible pulls, she is reading the situation and, although the story evades her, she can tell she's in the middle of it.

Jane arrives with Olivia and we regard each other, two women, keeping our eyes on faces, not skimming down bodies. Not like men do.

'Mae, this is Olivia. Olivia.' I repeat the new word clearly for my daughter.

'Bli-bi-a. Hello, Blibia!' Mae is trying her hardest to make the sounds. Her right palm outstretched towards this new friend.

'Why is she saying it like that?' Olivia is looking straight at Mae, but addressing someone else, her English accent more apparent than before. Her hands stay at her sides.

My heart lurches and my eyes fill. I glare at Steve – *CORRECT YOUR CHILD.*

'O-liv-i-a,' he says to Mae.

NOT THAT CHILD!

'She's just getting used to your name, that's all. She's never heard it before,' he says now. To the other, 'Well done, Mae.'

'It's a tricky name. You'll get it, darling,' I say. I feel motion-sick, swaying on a boat, nothing solid beneath me. 'O-liv-i-a.'

'Yes, Mama. Oooo-blib-i-a!'

'That's it!' I say, and smile. I put my hand to her face and feel steadier. She is my life raft. I take her still-empty, outstretched hand in mine.

'Three adults and two children, please.' Steve speaks through the open grille in the window.

'Your daughter gets a discount.'

'Sorry. I – they're both . . . Is it because she's under five?' He touches the top of Olivia's head.

'No, not that one. The other – that one.' Pointing at Mae. 'She gets in for half-price. Special-needs rate.' A nod. 'And one of you, too. An adult goes free because of her.'

Jane, Steve and I stand with painted smiles, waiting for our tickets. The half-price child and her full-price half-sister stand in front of us. The wristbands are printed and passed under the window. One is yellow and says 'SPECIAL' on it. And one of us gets to be free.

My husband walks ahead with Mae and Olivia, one on each side. He and I usually walk hand in hand, but now his hands are full. I want to give him something to hold so that he has to let go of Olivia. But then Mae motions me to take her free hand.

And we are Steve's three girls in a chain. Linked to him.

Jane walks behind us. I imagine her watching everything, taking it all in. I move carefully, smiling at the girls, glancing about me, interested in everything. So agreeable. The charming wife.

'What?' Steve says. My smiling has alarmed him.

I wonder if anyone were to look at us – and I'm sure they are because they always look and look again, wherever Mae is – would they ever guess the real story? That the girl without Down syndrome, the 'normal' one, the very image of her father, is where the real drama of this family lies.

How will Steve navigate this new responsibility? Will he be able to give enough of himself to each of these little girls? Will our daughter get the bigger straw? She absolutely needs it.

We stop at the monkeys and I lift Mae up to see, but then I hold her close. Close to me. I forget that she wants to see the monkeys.

'Mama?' She tilts her head and looks into my eyes. I haven't held her like this for a long time, up high, so tightly. She is seven. But right now she's not too old, and neither am I.

'You're the best girl in the world,' I say to her, as is my

habit. But today, when I say it, Steve doesn't smile. As is his habit. Instead, he looks flatly at me and turns away from us towards the monkeys.

We go into the zoo café and Steve joins the queue inside to order for us all, delighted with the chance to give his obliging side an airing in the present company. 'You guys find a table. I'll get this.'

Mr Big Stuff.

I take Mae's hand and stop at the first available table that will fit us all.

Jane tosses her head and looks around the room while Steve's gone. She sits up tall despite her height, accustomed to being noticed, to seeing herself reflected in the reactions of men, and then in their women. Even here in the poxy stinking zoo.

So we sit here – Jane and I and our respective daughters – two teams facing each other. Two women tolerating a trip to see animals in cages at the end of the earth to wring what they want from this life. From this man.

And lo! What have we here? He is coming towards us, all four pairs of eyes on him, and he managing two laden trays without complaining. 'I've got it! No problem!'

This is not my husband. Who is this congenial chap?

Oh, but he does prefer a different table, one just the same as this but a bit nearer the window. So we all get up, gather our things, take our wide smiles with us, and move. We all move again for him. We sit.

Yes, sir, yes, sir, three bags full.

There are two empty chairs remaining and he lowers himself onto the one beside Jane. She helps him with the trays, hands me my food. They are three now, facing us two.

He smiles and chats, is clownish with Mae, over-praises Olivia.

Jane makes a show of *really listening* to him. His words are strung like gaudy baubles between them. She laughs frequently and shakes her mane, keeping her side of the string up.

He touches the tip of Olivia's nose, leaves a blob of chocolate sauce on it. She giggles. Mae sees and wants to clean it for her. 'That's not where sauce goes, Dad!'

Olivia takes the napkin from Mae and does it herself.

My palms burn, itchy and sore, like chilblains.

I force his gaze to meet mine across the table. *Hello, Asshole. Remember me?*

I want it to be over. This day, to begin with, and then this whole nightmare. But she will probably outlive us all, being the youngest, being healthy. This storm will not pass. It has lifted us up, tossed our life into the air, and it's never going to put us down safely.

Only an inch or two separates my husband and his former lover, and there is a live intimacy between them that I tell myself I'm imagining. I cannot obsess, cannot scrutinise her now, not sitting facing them as I am.

Them.

They are bonded for ever. Olivia is their cement, and that fact sits like cement in my stomach.

'So, yes, I still work for Soloman's.' She says this to us both, and I can tell by the way she enunciates the company name that it carries weight, that it should mean something to me.

But I'm stuck on the *still*.

'They're Steve's company's main competitors, both out here and in Europe,' she elaborates, for me. Steve nods. 'We have pretty similar roles, actually,' she says then. He smiles at this. Similar roles. How lovely. 'I suppose it isn't very exciting to have only ever really worked in one place,' she goes on, and now it's her turn to smile, and Steve smiles again, and I join in, so we're all smiling, 'but then it's not so bad if you consider how well they pay me and that I'm only thirty-four.'

BOOM.

I want to say something clever, to fight her seemingly polite fire with a careful fire of my own, but I don't trust myself to speak and not throw petrol, with a match, at the whole table. So I take a breath. After a moment, I only manage a very delayed 'I see,' as my face burns. I lift my plastic cup to my cheeks to cool their heat. The dynamic between us has lurched yet again, with her side of the seesaw rising further into the sky. Well paid and young. I'm squat, knees bent, arse on the ground.

I excuse myself, but leave my bag and phone on the table between them. To remind them that I'll be right back.

I take Mae to the Ladies with me. And maybe I slam the

toilet door because I hear the bang as it bounces off its frame behind me. And when I look around, my daughter has her hands over her ears and is staring at me with wide eyes.

'So, where next for my girls?' He ruffles each one's hair, a hand on each dark head.

'Pen-wins! Dad, please?' Mae's soft voice.

'Penguins! That sounds *amaaaaazing*!' Steve mimes a penguin walking.

'I'd prefer to see the crocodiles next.' Olivia's voice is bold and confident.

'Crocodiles! Ooooh! Snap, snap!' Steve's arms open and close, chasing his daughters.

They smile and squeal up at him, their hero.

A wild river of jealousy runs through me. I feel it push up, trying to force its way out, reckless and ready to knock the things in its path.

But then those same crocodile arms are suddenly around my shoulders. And it confuses me. His arms, here, encircling me. The move is unexpected, complicates my rage. I want these arms: I want them here, just like this. My heart is thumping, and Jane is looking, and I lean into him, closing my eyes to everything just for a moment. And when I open them, I press my lips together and will them to stay dry.

Steve puts his hands on my cheeks, and they are warm. And love floods into my chest. His love is in demand now, so I feel this little win more keenly.

'Aaaaaaw,' says Mae, and squishes herself into us, hugs around our legs.

Olivia is watching. She frowns and puts her closed hand to her chin in a gesture that is all her father's. Evidence of an old betrayal, chipping at me.

'How much longer are we staying?' I ask quietly, now that Steve and I are close, his face next to mine. 'Maybe we can go after we've seen the penguins.'

Olivia walks towards the exit with Mae, while Jane is ahead of us all, leading the pack. My eyes are stuck on her shape in tight jeans. She is first out the gate and I know I can't keep up with her. But I can't allow myself to fall too far behind either. That would create space, leave a vacancy to be filled.

We give them a lift back to their hotel and Olivia says goodbye to us, to the whole car generally, while her mother says goodbye to my husband.

When we get home, Mae runs up the front lawn barefoot. I open the back door of the car and see her shoes and Olivia's flip-flops together on the floor.

* * *

'You kept this awful – this *secret* from me. I still can't even get my head around it, much less believe it.' Al is at the kitchen table, staring into his bowl of untouched cereal. 'The whole mess itself and the fact that I never knew. Never knew what you – did.'

Steve flinches. Puts his hand on our son's shoulder, trying to connect. 'Your mother knew, Al. And it was between us. Adult stuff. Within a marriage. It was nothing you should be involved in, buddy.'

'Well, I'm involved now! It has something to do with me now! You have another child, Dad. You have a child who lives on the other side of the world. So what about us? What about Mum and Mae? Who will take care of them now, when you're busy with her?'

'I will! What do you mean? Al, trust me, nothing has changed for us.' He smiles. 'For our family. The four of us. Your mother and I will work it out. You have nothing to worry about. It won't change how we are with each other.'

'You can't actually believe that, Dad.'

'We love each other and we are a family, Al. And we always will be.' He nods, convincing himself and our son of the impenetrable simplicity of being *a family*.

'That's such crap. This is the real world and obviously I know Mum better than you do. And I know how she feels about you. I know how much of herself she gives to us, and I know what family actually means to her. And it isn't this.' He waves his hand around the room. 'It isn't another woman and a child and everything being dismissed as "no worries". She won't be able to be cool with this. How the hell do *you* need *me* to tell you that?'

I listen in the doorway, full of heartache and pride.

* * *

Jane has a way of meeting everyone's gaze. Of being surrounded by people and fearless in the face of them all.

Hello. Look at me.

Her eyes are always busy, grabby. They seem to grow as she listens to Steve talk while mine narrow into slits. I can still see out enough to notice the nest she's building between us.

I study her. And she sees me. She doesn't smile, just looks back.

Hello.

Hiya.

Stalemate.

I sulk and snap at Steve, knowing I'm doing her work for her, making myself look like a shrew. But I can't stop.

* * *

All three of us are watching where ground is being lost and gained. Jane, Steve and I.

Three and a half weeks to go. Who will win? And is there a prize?

Of course, everyone will lose.

As if she can sense me thinking about her just then, Jane appears at my front door. But I think about her most of the time. So there's nothing remarkable in this. It's not even a coincidence, more of an inevitability, really.

'Another glorious bright day!' she says. 'How could anyone be in bad form with a November like this?'

She is young, even for her age. Her statements and questions are all certain, loud.

Fucking annoying, actually.

But the heart has a blind spot, so all Steve sees is Olivia's mother. And that makes her wondrous. Of course, she is also not-the-wife, which gives her an advantage over me in terms of allure. Isn't that the human condition? To desire what is not certain. My father would say so.

Steve might too. If he were honest.

'Tell me this, Beth, do you ever miss the rain and the stone buildings?' she asks me now. 'The dilapidation of Dublin, old pubs and all that religion. Ugh!' She gives a little theatrical shudder. 'How wonderful to have had this chance in life – to be free of all of that.'

'I do miss it, actually,' I say.

'No, you don't!' She laughs. 'Really?'

'The humour, the grit of the place, the culture, the history. And even the skies full of rolling clouds. I do, yes.' I think about winter evenings back home, the rain coming down like cold gravel, the yellow moon and the darkness so complete it's like velvet, and then our front door, Christmas-tree lights and an open fire, sitting in an armchair listening for the weather and wondering about snow, while music plays low and raindrops lengthen on the window panes. I do miss it. The embrace of it.

Everything is bright here now, coming into blossom. Another sunrise, another sunset – the days warming and getting longer. But, for the first time, I'm wishing they would end. I count them down like a prisoner. Twenty-five to go. Until she fucks off home. So that Steve and I can begin again.

'Oh, come on. I bet you don't miss a thing.' She stretches her long legs out, runs her hands down them. 'I know I wouldn't. I could live here easily.' Her voice is a drawl, her words drawn out like the evenings. 'Never go back to England.'

I hold my fire. Twenty-five days to go.

* * *

Steve's sleeping a lot now, his body and mind shutting down to the stubborn chaos of our lives. Well, I should say that when he's around *me*, he's sleeping a lot. Closing his eyes, keeping himself back, tidied away.

* * *

'I've never known anyone involved in a paternity test before,' Claire says. 'You're like one of those daytime TV families everyone admires so much.'

'Thanks. I'm really proud of it.'

'I can imagine.'

I didn't need to see any DNA profiling. The evidence had been sitting at my kitchen table the previous day, pressing down hard on a glittery sticker, her fingernails flat and square, just like Steve's.

'He tells me it was a shag. Nothing.'

87

'I think that's most certainly true, Beth.'

'Maybe it was nothing then but it's not now. What is Jane to him now? And what does she want?'

'Why don't you ask her?'

* * *

Steve expects me to do everything, to be the hostess of the glass house, the way I would if this were an ordinary dinner, if these were ordinary guests coming around for a bite to eat, to catch up. Cloth napkins, flowers, jugs of iced water with cucumber slices, a playlist chosen. But I look at him and my expression reminds him of just what is going on here, and how not-ordinary it is. He stands up and asks if he can help with anything.

'You're sure she said this evening?' I say. Jane and Olivia are ten minutes late and I'm on a knife edge already without it turning out that they're not late at all – that we're actually twenty-four hours early. 'You're sure it's not tomorrow evening?'

I can't face the prospect of doing very little for them and feeling both guilty and livid about it, all over again.

'Yes. Well, I think so . . .' He rummages in his pocket for his mobile. He stands there, checking his texts from Jane. What a world. Wives entertaining husbands, their old lovers and the children they created during an off-period.

I walk around the kitchen putting things back, taking things out. Everything is hunky-dory. But he's still scrolling, scrolling down and down.

'Surely you know when we were to have your ex-lover and her daughter over for dinner with our children.'

His face looks slapped.

'Sorry, Steve. Sorry. It's just such a—'

He puts his phone down, places his arms around me. They're warm and smell of sun lotion, and I feel my edges start to soften. 'I know. The whole situation is expecting a lot of you. And of Al. I know that. And I love you so much for having them here. It's huge. Maybe Al will feel a bit better about things after this evening.'

And just then, while we're embracing, Jane comes up the steps, walks in, killing it. She is wearing the get-up of a woman intent on stopping conversations – tight jeans and a top made of interlocking metal hoops and white cotton. Her hair is pulled back into a high and swinging ponytail.

Olivia is beside her in a peach-coloured sundress, barefoot, her long dark hair loose and free. Her dress is the floaty kind with big pockets that I don't buy for Mae because it doesn't come up high enough at the chest to hide her scar. The pale blush ridge starts at her navel and climbs to her neckline, a reminder of heart surgery that split her in two to keep her alive. The scar is a medal of bravery, but one she can never choose to unpin. It's a mark of horror too. Always drawing the eye, always speaking up for her. I've come to prefer crew necks these days anyway.

But, then, I suppose that's what mothers of heart-children do.

A shot of feeling, naked, like jealousy, darts through me. For Mae. I think.

I call her to help me set the table, just so Jane and Olivia will see that she can. And so that Steve will be proud of her. And maybe of me a bit too.

Mae's careful little hands judge the spaces between the chairs and place the cutlery just so. When she lays the final knife down, I have to stop myself looking over at the others for approval. Instead I look at her, my daughter, and in that moment her almond eyes hold mine with a kind of knowing. She smiles at me and her face outshines everything else in the room. 'We're a good team,' she says.

'The best,' I answer, touching her cheek, her light.

Olivia and Mae are chasing each other around the back garden, squealing with delight. Also outside now, the early-evening sun shining down on her, up-for-anything Jane is playing the funster to my bucket of water. Our glass doors are pulled back so far that even their frames have disappeared into themselves, leaving everything on show. I look out to the garden and see her bouncing on our trampoline. Her arms stretched straight above her are stabbing the air, her breasts bouncing to her chin, her laughter bouncing in here through the spaces where the doors should be and off our wooden floors – *ha ha ha*. Bounce bounce bounce. I am in the kitchen, sorting and fixing. I am the sensible older woman, house-bound and guarded, while Jane risks the great outdoors and says a big YES to everything the world has to offer. Everything my world has to offer.

I want to set her on fire.

I see what she's doing: she's being exactly the kind of woman that Steve doesn't even know he wants. Reading him. The nothing-is-a-problem, cool and exuberant kind that doesn't exist beyond the courtship stage. She appears wholly innocent – just so much fun! – to a weak man or a bystander. Unless that bystander is an already-burned wife.

Obviously it might be prudent for me to be kind, supportive, a good partner – as a younger model may be waiting in my husband's wings. And obviously he and I should see this through together, should get through these weeks as a team.

But, right now, I am utterly fucked off. And that's obvious too. There are no two ways about it, and there's no single way to hide it.

I take the lid off the pot in the centre of the table and we all smile at the minimal-effort, kids' favourite, pasta-Bolognese affair inside. The way a happy family on TV might.

Mae gives an *Ooooooh!* as the steam rises, which makes Olivia laugh.

I call Al and his bedroom door opens immediately. He must have been standing right behind it.

Steve stacks a mountain of barbecued burgers on a dish to one side.

Would she have had sex with him if she'd known Mae had Down syndrome? If she'd known his stakes were so high?

That's what I'm thinking as I spoon pasta onto Jane's plate. I look into her face.

Probably.

My husband makes a fist of starting a round-table conversation by saying something innocuous about the weather today. Usually this is my role. When he stops speaking, Jane recognises the cue and says something back. Just words. Whatever. Anything. Steve nods along. I know he's already panicking over his next turn.

A moment later silence falls, the quiet laden with unsaid things. Who will be first to go where the wild things are?

The scrape of cutlery against my plate as I move food around.

Steve pours wine. Pretends to read the label, the vintage. Looks vaguely satisfied by the year, knowing nothing. I feel I should make a joke, throw him a raft. But I don't, and the awkward moments drag by, stretching themselves across the table, taut.

Mae and Olivia make faces at each other and giggle. I smile at my daughter. I feel Steve's eyes on me, so I look around the room, casually, anywhere but at him. I'm a grown woman behaving like a pissed-off grown woman.

He puts his hand on my leg under the table. He wants to keep me onside so I'll be good-humoured, chatty. I glance at Jane and see she is looking at him. I sigh, but not as loudly as I want to. The art of compromise.

He breathes in and sits up taller.

'Beth and I used to live in London, actually,' he says to Jane, apropos of nothing, starting a limp conversation that he hopes we'll all slither into.

Al sighs, more obviously than I did.

Jane smiles, nods, cuts her burger into elegant pieces, eats delicately. She is ice cool, sure of her position. She has a permanent place at Steve's table in the shape of his perfect daughter.

'I don't like this kind of pasta. I don't want it,' the perfect daughter whines.

Her mother speaks to her firmly and politely: 'Olivia, darling, you can have this or a burger. Which would you like?'

'I don't like those burgers either. They're all black.'

'They're supposed to be like that. They're delicious. So, you can have some pasta or you can have a yummy burger or . . .' Jane motions at the tabletop, at the couple of bowls of salad and some bread '. . . or else you can go hungry.'

'I don't like any of it.'

Steve looks at me and I know that this is where I should suggest some alternative, should cobble together a few snacks on a plate for her. Even some crisps or chopped fruit. But I don't. Mae is eating pasta shells that she has speared along her fork. Her free hand is patting Olivia's arm gently.

'Didn't we, Beth?' Steve says, after the interruption has passed and along with it another stretch of near-unbearable silence. 'Used to live in London?'

'We did, yes,' I tell my own husband. 'We moved just after Al was born,' I elaborate to him, then look around the table. 'And we stayed for seven years,' I sing-song obediently.

He ignores my tone and simply agrees with me. 'Yes, seven.'

The air is sticky with impolite tension.

Why did she decide to cut herself out of the photo she sent? Why didn't she make the small effort and just take a picture of the child alone?

She actually managed to get herself both into and out of the photo.

My mind is sawing backwards and forwards, cutting through things known and unknown. I'm pinned, unable to say anything real.

Was she saving her blonde hair and big boobs as a surprise for me?

Jane is talking about being at the beach with Olivia that morning, how much they enjoyed it. *Blah-blah-blah.*

Her daughter just sits, examining the burger on her plate. Scraping at the top of it.

Al hasn't looked up from his plate once.

Anger floods through me, at this invasion, this woman, this upheaval.

Sex.

Olivia is seated next to Steve. He lifts his arm now and rests it along the back of the chair. He looks at me. I return the look. He leaves his arm across the back. We are two people in a still from a play. Neither of us moving, but our guns are in our holsters.

Olivia forgets about her food sulk and tells him about a new purple bag she got for starting pre-school. Mae listens, smiling. Steve wears the expression of a man ready to make promises.

Jane refills Steve's water glass and touches his hand as she does it.

Al glances at me. 'The burgers are good, Mum,' he says.

'They are,' I say. 'Your father did them a different way this evening.'

Al gives a short laugh. And then his voice is loud and sudden: 'Sorry, but I actually can't sit here any longer.' My son throws down his cutlery and slaps both of his hands onto the table, one each side of his plate. 'You're okay with this, Mum, are you? You're okay with Dad and this woman—'

'Her name is Jane,' Steve says foolishly.

'Yes, thanks for that, Dad. I KNOW WHAT HER NAME IS.' Al doesn't take his eyes from mine as he answers his father.

'You're okay, Mum? With THIS WOMAN' – still no name, but Steve says nothing now – 'in your home? With Dad?'

He is young, the world is unjust, his father has fallen. He addresses me again, with the might of his loyalty. 'You don't think you deserve better than this? Because you absolutely do.'

My heart is soaring now seeing him, hearing him. And yet it's breaking too. The unit is collapsing. And I won't be able to fix it. Steve isn't the only man in the room. And our son is right – I do deserve better. I know that.

But I'm afraid. I'm afraid of losing everything if I upturn the table, if I lay down the law. I am afraid of losing Steve to her again.

How long have I been afraid, been so uncertain of what we have?

I look around the room. Everything is where it was, nothing has changed. And yet nothing looks the same as it did three weeks ago, before Jane and Olivia arrived. The light falls differently, barely falls at all – or is it just that the shine has gone? Everything has been scuffed and marked as though someone has taken a wire brush to the room, to us. Scratched at our veneer with long, careless sweeps.

I've been afraid for over four years. Since his night with her.

How easily we have been uncovered. How quickly I have become undone.

'Al! Please.' Steve's voice is raised. 'We have guests. Have some respect—'

'Don't you talk to me about respect. Some family man you are.' Al snorts, looking at him for the first time. 'Is this enough family for you?' With his arm, he motions around the room. A little sea of stunned faces.

Olivia gets up and goes to her mother. Leans into her.

My son reaches out to Mae, puts his hand to her cheek.

96

His voice changes entirely. 'Mae, sweetie, you should take Olivia out to play in the garden. I'll come out in a minute and we'll have a game on the trampoline. Okay?'

She looks around the table, then back to him. Smiles at him. Trust. 'T-ball?'

'Whatever you like.'

'Come on, Blibia. Let's go.' She gets down from her chair. 'Love you, Mama,' she says, looking into my face, as she passes slowly.

Silence and smiles now from the adults until the girls have left the room.

'Al. We can talk about this ourselves later, my love.' My voice is tender, my hand on his arm.

'No!' he shouts, a spring snapping. 'I want you to talk about it now.' He brings his fist down on the table, causing water to slosh over the side of his full glass. 'Sorry, Mum,' he says more quietly, looking at the spill. 'But I've had enough. Enough for me and for Mae. And for you.'

'Okay.' I jump in before Steve does. 'The thing is, honey, we have to deal with the situation. And, really, I don't see that we have much choice—'

'Well, that's just not true. I'm only nineteen and even I know that. There's always choice. And you three need to talk about your options now and work this shit out.' He pushes his chair back from the table and stands, towering over us. 'Get to some kind of an honest resolution. Please.'

And then he leaves, goes outside to his sister. And the other one. 'Mae! You big legend. What are you at?'

His voice joyful, he is able to play the game. 'That's not bouncing! *This* is bouncing.'

The glorious sound of my daughter's laughter.

'He'll come round,' Steve says, taking my hand. 'Rightly or wrongly, this is the road and we're all on it.'

Jane shifts in her seat.

'Wrongly, Steve. It's wrongly. And surely there's more to life than quiet perseverance. Even our teenage son knows that. I do deserve better.'

Out of my eye-line, Jane mouths, 'Oh dear,' to my husband. But because she doesn't know as much as she thinks she does, and that includes the layout of our kitchen, she doesn't know that I've seen her doing it, reflected in the mirror opposite.

But Steve does. Steve knows better, knows more. And his eyes meet mine in that mirror.

Heat roars into my face.

'I think it's time for you to go now, Jane.' My voice is loud and steady. 'We'll talk again over the next day or two.' I twist my hand around Steve's – *STAY WHERE YOU ARE*.

'Do you think it's—'

'I do, honey, yes.' I answer a question that he may not have been posing. 'I definitely think it's time.'

Jane stands and gathers up her bag, her keys. She brings her glass to her lips.

Steve and I wait. He gives a single cough.

She puts the glass back on the table and says a jolly

'Okay, then.' Her lipstick has left a kiss mark behind. 'Liv, darling! Come here, please.'

And then Olivia and Mae are in the room, all giddiness and laughter and chasing in circles. They slow down and stand facing each other, their hands clapping and meeting as they chant a rhyme.

Reflected in each other. Similar colouring. Similar heights, despite the age difference. Because of the age difference. A fairground mirror, one that distorts. Shows you what might have been.

'We have to go now, Liv,' Jane says.

'But, Muuuuuum, I don't want to! I've not finished playing,' Olivia whinges.

'Well, I'm afraid we have to.' Her voice is kind. She is the good witch.

Olivia frowns at me, knowing I am the party killer. Mae looks at me now too, takes her new friend's hand. 'Come the next day!' she says. My daughter trying to keep a friend. 'Come back and we'll play again. Don't be sad.'

Steve bends to their level and says he'll take them somewhere special during the week.

They listen, their dark eyes fixed on him.

Olivia takes the iPod they were using for music outside from her pocket and hands it back to me. I wipe her fingerprints from the little screen. She brings out my mother in me.

Steve runs his hands through his hair.

'Can Blibia stay for sleepover next time? Pleeeeeease, Mum? Can she?'

And so it happens that I am walking between Steve and Jane as we go down our driveway in the dark. One of them each side of me, and Olivia behind. Escorting me to the edge of a cliff.

And then Jane and Olivia drive away. I am spared, for now.

'Blibia's my best friend,' Mae announces, as Steve and I come back into the kitchen.

Al is leaning against the sink. He looks at us, shaking his head.

'Beth and I used to live in London, actually.' I mimic Steve's voice back at him, when we're upstairs and alone.

'What would you have had me say?'

'How about "What are you doing here? What was wrong with the telephone? What THE FUCK do you want?" Al is dead right. Sort it out.' I am shout-whispering, livid but not wanting to waken my children. Even my fury is restricted, I think, while my voice rasps out of me.

'Well, there was no need for you to be so frosty with her, in any event. You pretty much kicked the woman out of our home.'

'Pardon?' I had heard.

'I'm just saying that you were unnecessarily cool—'

'I was unnecessarily cool with your lover who came

around for dinner and started mouthing little messages at you when she thought I couldn't see?' I give a mean laugh. 'You get pissed off if one of my exes sends my parents a Christmas card.'

'You're seeing something in nothing, Beth. Nothing. The smallest things. People smile, you know. People chat. It doesn't mean anything other than getting along, doing their best.'

'Okay, Steve, so you fucked a stranger – I had to get over that – and then it turned out that you and the stranger had a child together. Great. And now that I've just about managed to absorb that fact, you want me to welcome them into our family. You want me to chat to them, to laugh with them, to share stories around the dinner table about our life before them, where we lived, what we did. And you expect the same of Al and Mae. That they will accept your other family as part of ours. You're living in a fucking fantasy land.'

'Fine! Forget it! I'm the cheat so I deserve nothing from my family.' He is shout-whispering now too. 'I'm the bad man, the bad husband, so you guys don't need to support me at all. Even when I'm in crisis. Olivia is living proof of just how bad I am. Fine. I'll never expect anything from you or the kids again and – just so we're clear – I'll never be able to apologise enough for what I did.'

'You could give it a fucking try.'

'I'M SORRY! I'M SO SORRY. FUCK.'

And then he sits on the edge of the bed and the room is silent.

'And yet . . .'

I wince. Wow. That didn't take long.

'And YET! She is here and she is mine.' His voice breaks. 'And she is just a girl. A little girl. And I am her father. And I hate the mess it causes but – can you understand? Can you even just try to, for me? Just for a moment, please try to understand that it's hard for me to look at her and not see something good.'

My heart clenches because that part I can understand.

'I imagine you playing with her hair,' I say later, the words coming from somewhere dark and honest inside me.

'What?'

'I imagine it. You playing with her long hair. Jane's hair.'

'Beth – stop. Please. You're tormenting yourself. It wasn't like that. It was nothing. It wasn't – *romantic*.'

The novelty of it, splayed across the pillow, spreading out, around her face. A mermaid sinking into the sea.

'I love you, Beth. Just you. Okay?'

I look into his face, his eyes, for something real to latch on to. An anchor.

'You'll feel better in the morning,' he says, kissing my forehead.

I doubt it. At least when it's night, I know that he's by my side. Mornings bring all kinds of possibilities. And then so many hours in these long days. All that scope for mistrust.

I want the nights to go on for ever.

I move across so I am lying behind him. He leans back a little and opens his arm to curve it around me, to pull me towards him. We sleep.

When we waken in the morning, he smiles at me. 'We're in the same boat, Bethy,' he says quietly.

'Yes, I know,' I answer. *Your boat.*

* * *

'Why must she interfere so thoroughly, darling? Be so *present* in your life.' My mother's face fills my iPad. 'The child is one thing, but *her mother*,' the last two words said with venom, 'is an entirely different matter as she is unrelated to us all, in every possible way.'

'Her daughter is only three and a half, Mum, and Steve is, as yet, a stranger to her.' I defend the situation to myself as much as to my mother. 'So Jane has to be around too.'

'I don't know. I think it's all a bit fishy, I don't mind telling you. Is there more to this? To Steve and this woman? All I'd want to know is when exactly she's leaving.'

'Only a couple of weeks left to get through now. And I suppose it's right that Steve and I just get on with things. Embrace it, for the children's sake.'

'Only a couple of weeks. And then the rest of your lives.' She tuts loudly. 'I don't like it, you being expected to sit with this woman, to have her in your house. I simply wouldn't have it. Steve had better not be making her feel too welcome. Even Annabel wondered at her level of *involvement*.'

I put my hands over my face and drag my cheeks down.

An affair! A child! A second *girl*! Of course the news had made it across the world, shock propelling it along at high speed. Naturally Annabel and the rest of the golf club would have an opinion.

'Don't do that, darling. You look hideous.'

Steve walks through the room behind me, and my mother's head snaps in his direction. 'Is this woman trying to hinder your marriage, Steven?' She speaks very loudly, and doesn't wait for an answer. 'Because I think she is, and I also think it is very much my business, even though I imagine you don't. My daughter's happiness and that of my grandchildren. Well, that's always going to absolutely be my business. Even if you did move them all *out there*.' Her mouth – even on the small screen – is set in a very visible line when she finishes her monologue.

Steve had kept walking throughout.

I can't hear you.

He is gone now.

* * *

'You're making this more difficult than it needs to be, Beth.'

'I'm not *making* it anything. It just is. All by itself. It just *is* fucking difficult.'

'I know it is, I know that. But you're acting like I wanted all of this to happen.'

'I'm not, but I must say that you do seem pretty happy with yourself when you've been with them. With Olivia.'

'Well, I am, yes, in a way – but that's because she's here now and I'm trying to enjoy some time with her. She's *my child*.'

'I swear to God, Steve, if you say *my child* in that pious tone once more— A shag in a hotel while your wife and kids are at home does not a father make.'

It was a shitty thing to say, which was why I said it.

* * *

Mae takes my face in her little hands to steady me, so I can see into her eyes, so she can see into mine. Her emotional antennae have tuned in to me and are not happy with what they've found. She strokes my face with her hand until my thoughts slow down.

And they do.

She is still and patient and I am her only focus. I want to weep at this, at the honest love between us.

I smile at her. A real smile. Not like the ones I've been faking lately. I'm still alive, still vital. She has reminded me.

* * *

We make love, Steve and I. That is to say, we fuck. It's not rough or angry – it's just physical. A need. Neither romantic nor resentful. Just physical. The way that sex between strangers can be. And then we roll apart.

* * *

'Olivia and Jane aren't going to fade away, Beth.'

'I know that.' They both have too much colour. I am the one fading. 'What is it you really want, Steve?'

He is standing rubbing his lower back. 'I just want my children – all of them – to be happy and confident. You know? And ambitious in life. My priorities haven't changed at all. They're the same as always. It's just that I want those things for Olivia now too. As I want them for Al.' He pauses for a minute, his tongue bulging in his cheek as he thinks of them. His wants. And then: 'And for Mae, of course. But that's a bit different. Obviously.'

Obviously.

'Surely having me in her life might help my daughter towards her goals one day. You know, in some way?'

He means Olivia. Olivia's life. Olivia's goals. And while his voice is gentle, I know his resolve is iron-clad.

I say nothing but stand next to him, then sidle in under the crook of his arm to convince myself that I still belong there. To check if we still fit.

'Olivia will be starting school in a year or so,' he goes on, 'and Jane wants her to understand – to have the full picture – about her parents before then, so she knows who she is.'

Her parents. I could hear Jane's words being repeated

back to me. 'I see. But a few trips for ice-cream doesn't make you a parent, Steve,' I say quietly. 'You know that.'

'I do.' He tucks my hair behind my ear. 'Being a parent does. Which is why I'm going to be that. Be present. Parent.' The last word is said as a verb.

My blood is pumping in my neck and thumping into my chest, and I hope that he can't feel it – feel this pulsing wife under his arm, struggling to keep her breath even, her most vital wishes beating against his.

Be present.

* * *

I tilt my head to his when he leaves for work, but my kisses are dry and flat. I watch him walk out to the car, whistling on his way.

Before, I saw a man who was content, positive, doing his best.

Now I look at him and think, *God, he's full of himself.*

* * *

How could a little girl be trouble?

With brown eyes and plaits of black hair, that's how.

* * *

I never felt real loneliness before I met Steve. I've always taken that to mean I must love him. He has the power to make me lonely. Only love can break a heart, and all that.

Isn't that how you know it's love? Or is that just loneliness?

Steve tells me about his morning with Olivia and I hold myself tightly, barely breathing, to stop myself shouting out. I don't know how any movement or sound might go, so best not make one at all. Any reaction might cause him to stop talking or to filter his words. And I need to know all the words. To have the whole picture. Every nauseating brushstroke. Because otherwise Jane will know more than I do. And I've had more than enough of that.

I can't have him unreadable again. Inaccessible. He would be lost to me.

* * *

'He told me to learn from this, to see how mistakes are made and to try to be better than him. Can you believe that?'

Al is next to me, but avoiding my eyes, looking out into the garden.

'I felt like I could punch him. Me! Punching someone! I've never felt that way before in my life. And it's Dad. Of all the people in the world, the only one I want to punch is my father.' He shakes his head. *'Be better than me, Al. That's actually what he said.* As though I needed this example – this Olivia, on the fringes of my life for ever – to realise that cheating isn't ideal.'

'What did you say?'

'I said I already was.'

* * *

108

'Mae really seems to like Olivia, don't you think?' Steve says.

'Mae likes most people.'

'Well, I know, but even so, I'm glad. Glad that they get along.'

'Mae doesn't know who she is. The walls around her mind don't allow this kind of . . .' I cast about me, waving my arms, for a word '. . . *complexity* in. I think she'd feel differently about her, and about you for that matter, if she did get how all of this happened.'

I wonder if she'll ever get it. If she thinks really hard about it, some day, when she's a bit older.

'So Mae only likes her because she's *impaired*? Is that what you're saying, Beth?'

'Well, Al doesn't have an intellectual disability. How do you think he likes her?'

* * *

'The child is managing to get in everywhere,' I say to Claire. 'She's seeping through the cracks.'

Claire listens.

'And, God knows, there's enough cracks between Steve and me now. There isn't enough paper in the world to cover them. Until recently, I didn't even know this little girl existed. Now every time I turn around, she seems to be standing there. I know about her chipping her front tooth the morning she was due to start at crèche, about her allergy to strawberries, about how she was a week overdue when she was born.'

'A week overdue? Lazy cow,' Claire says, smiling.

'And Steve allows himself to be persuaded by her. Like he does with Mae.' I rub my eyes. 'But naturally I like it when it happens with Mae.'

Claire sips her tea, letting me talk.

'She's so confident too. For such a young child, who is far from home and suddenly has a father.' I sigh loudly. 'And I'm pretty sure that Steve sees his life as just a series of snares – me, Ireland, now all of this and he's stuck with—'

'Maybe he should stop walking into them, then. These snares,' Claire says curtly. 'Look, Beth,' her voice softens, and she puts her cup down, 'you love him, but do you still want to be with him?'

'I want to have his love, and to love him back. Is that selfish? To want to know that I'm the only one in his orbit?'

'No, it's not.'

'I actually feel itchy around her – Jane bothers me so much that I want to scratch at myself. Is that as crazy as it sounds? Like my skin is alive with jealousy. I know Steve likes her, and why wouldn't he? She's fun, she's lovely to him and she's beautiful to look at.' A sadness sweeps over me so I keep talking to stop it settling. 'She sat on our chair by the doorway – you know the white antique one we had restored? The one that nobody ever dreams of fucking sitting on? Well, she walked in on Thursday evening and sat herself there. And it bothered me so much. I can't even explain it. *Nobody* sits on that chair. But, of course, Jane does. A decorative antique chair. God. I know I really need to calm down but something in her makes me wild.'

'Your husband,' Claire says. 'It's your husband in her that makes you wild.'

I laugh despite myself. 'Yes, there is that. Although I'd like to think I've moved on from that slightly. What probably bothers me most is that there's this air of victory about her – in the midst of all of this wreckage and chaos.'

'I'd want to throw the chair at her.'

'I actually considered putting it upstairs, once she'd left. How ridiculous is that? Taking the chair upstairs so it wouldn't be there for her the next time.'

'That sounds like a plan, were it not for the fact that you risk ending up with no furniture at all downstairs before the end of her trip.'

'Or maybe she'd sit in my chair then. Which would be worse.'

'Or Steve's.'

'Ugh.'

'With him.'

'Okay, stop! The chair stays.'

Claire leans towards me. 'Beth, everything stays. She goes. You'll see. Ride it out. She will leave here soon, as planned. For the other side of the world. And, anyway, you and Steve have twenty years together. She can't compete with that.'

'I think what's new often has the edge. A lot of men are distracted by what's shiny. Like beady magpies.'

Like he was, before.

One for sorrow.

'Regardless of everything, you are *not* competing with this woman for your own husband.'

Oh, but I am. Over the years, I've felt something in my shadow from time to time, but trying to identify it or even acknowledging it would have made my life less possible. Fear. But now, here's Jane coming up the outside, checking her phone for his messages. A shiny distraction, and the embodiment of my fear.

* * *

I arrive home and there are two cups in the sink. I leave them there. In case I want to ask about them later. But then I don't want him to remember using them, to remember their tea time, so I go back to the kitchen and put them in the dishwasher.

* * *

Getting out of my car in our front garden, I hear my husband's low laughter. I come into the house and see he is alone, just on the phone. I breathe out. Relax.

He raises a finger to me – *just a minute.* 'I know! Yes, she is.' He is smiling, animated. 'She is! And actually I do know where she gets that – my mother used to do the same.'

He laughs again in a way that he hasn't laughed with me in weeks. Nothing I say makes him laugh like that any more.

While I stand there, he mouths, 'Sorry,' to me, points at the phone, and leaves to continue the conversation upstairs.

* * *

'I was hoping that . . .'

Lately, Steve seems to start every sentence the same way. 'I was hoping that . . .' followed by whatever today's request might be. As though all that matters to everyone is what he is hoping for and how we might all juggle our work and schedules so he can achieve whatever he has just imagined.

He uses any time he's actually at home planning what he'd like to do next.

Or sleeping.

'I was hoping that . . .

1. . . . we might all bring Olivia to see the caves this afternoon.'
2. . . . I could spend a couple of hours after lunch at the park with Olivia and Mae and then bring them back here. Just us. If you have anything to do, you know, *out* somewhere.'
3. . . . I could take Olivia for a drive on my way home from the office, out to see where I grew up.'
4. . . . I might spend the day out on the boat. Alone. I need some headspace.'

Well, I was hoping you might fuck off on the boat and take Olivia with you.

But not Jane. Leave her where I can see her.

I mention Mae's speech-therapy appointment and he nods, making sounds of vague agreement. It's clear to both of us that he hasn't a clue and that he believes he's hearing about it for the first time. I hope this is because his head is full of Olivia. Because otherwise it's full of her mother.

* * *

I'm coming down our hallway when I overhear Jane speaking: 'Did you manage to resolve that issue with the guy at work?'

'Yeah, actually,' Steve answers. 'Sorry for bending your ear about that. Things are a bit better with him these last couple of days.'

And this simple exchange feels like the worst moment of all. Of everything that has happened over the last few weeks. And I give in to the tears filling my eyes. Because standing there against the wall, out of sight in my own life, I have no idea what they're talking about.

Later that night, in the still darkness of our bedroom, I can't bring myself to ask him what had been bothering him at work, or to ask why he didn't share it with me, because I know I will cry in the asking.

* * *

The following evening I hear him come in but don't greet him in the kitchen this time. I run upstairs so he has to come and find me. I rationalise that these first moments are important. That they are when the balance of power for the remaining hours of the day is established, the mood set down, the arm of today's victor raised into the air.

Don't go to him. Let him come for you. By the time I stop myself and wonder where I learned this rubbish, I'm already up in our bedroom with the door closed so I just stay where I am.

I am my mother, hiding cups, not asking questions, and now trying to win battles with foolish manoeuvres.

But then Steve appears, wondering if I'm okay. 'I thought you weren't home. I couldn't find you.' He sits next to me on the bed. Close and gentle.

And I think, *Mother – what big wiles you have.*

But, then, is everything just a game?

* * *

I am standing in my back garden, looking into my house through its glass walls, watching a domestic scene. A dark man and a blonde woman in the lounge, two daughters playing upstairs. The woman is sitting on my couch with her legs drawn up beneath her, her wedge heels kicked off and lying sideways on the rug. I imagine that later she will lean on the crook of the man's arm for balance while she puts them back on. The man is standing, talking, the woman looking up at him with her whole face: each of his words is a marvel.

I want to knock on the window. Loudly. Maybe smash it.

They are in my house, living my life, Jane in my place, Steve barely noticing the change. I watch through glass. Deposed.

I come in, open the fridge door, lean against it, look in at nothing, pick at things on the shelves. Their conversation peters into polite nothings behind my back. I linger in front of some cold meats.

Are they waiting for me to leave? To leave my kitchen, to leave this mad house?

I shut the fridge and flick through a newspaper that's been on the kitchen table since this morning. I stop and hold my breath in the quiet. Nothing stirs.

I look at a stain that's marked the worktop for at least a year. Maybe from a hot dish or a pan. I could get at it with a lemon and some baking soda. Or I could take a hammer to the whole kitchen.

Jane's chair makes a sudden scraping noise along the floor as she excuses herself and goes to the bathroom.

* * *

It is Olivia now who makes Steve happiest. When he is with her, his face softens. He is all hugs and smiles and gentleness. She gets the best of him. Mae, Al and I get the tired version.

116

'We're not partners any more,' I say.

'We are.'

'Okay, so let's say we are—'

'Yes, let's. Because it's true.'

'Okay, but now there's a third partner. Another adult. Another *parent* in our relationship. And it already feels like we can't make decisions without considering her. We – you and I, our life together – have been *interrupted* and—'

'It's you and me, Beth. You know that. Always. We can decide things together, and *tell* Jane.'

'Steve, she is Olivia's *mother*. You will not be dictating her child's needs, I can guarantee you that.'

'We're the team, Beth. You and I, Al and Mae.' He smiles at me. 'Team Rogers, honey.'

'And Olivia? Is she the team captain?'

He doesn't reply.

'Okay, so who am I to Olivia?'

'You're – well, you're my wife. So you're her father's wife.' Steve smiles uncertainly, picking back through his words, trying to read my face, assessing if I want to be more or less.

'What does it make *me*, though? What does *she* make *me*, Steve?' *Other than crazy.*

A wagon, he probably wants to say.

* * *

The power of poetry to sum things up when ordinary

117

language won't do. The language of crisis. Writing about what's under my nose. Trying to find the beauty – or even the truth – in this bloody nightmare.

I sit down to write but it's maddening, not therapeutic at all. The letters fling themselves at the page, the nib of the pen leaving scrapes on the paper, carving up the lines. I feel worse. It's too soon, too now. Everything is rushing from me at once, too much.

'Read it for me, Beth,' Steve says.

'I don't want – it's nothing yet. Not ready, really.'

'Please. Whatever you have. Read it for me.'

'Well, it's—'

'For me. Go on.'

He doesn't want to hear it as much as he wants me to do as he asks. Spoiled. Everything about him. I'm being tested, not on the poem but on how much I care what he wants.

'Please.'

'Okay.'

I look at the page in front of me but don't read a single word from it. Instead I open my mouth and 'The Beadsman' comes out. A poem I wish I'd written. Words I want him to hear.

'And you?
The years,
What did they bring?
And were you filled?

Was it enough?
And would you go that way again?
Almost a lifetime we have lived apart.
And they who brought me news are long dead now.
They said you'd found a quiet town,
quite near the sea, and settled down.
I think of this.
Of the salt on your lips.
The years go by so quickly here.
The days.
And I have learned to lean against the pull.
It is a small pain now, but I shall not lose it.
And all is well, and I wish you well.'

C.P. Stewart's words, not mine.

And so, in a small way, we both win.

And I have learned to lean against the pull.

'Wow. I like it,' he says.

'*And would you go that way again?*' I repeat the line to him.

He is quiet for a moment, then clears his throat and looks down at the sports pages. 'It's great, Beth. Really. I'd leave it as it is.' His voice is low. 'As it is.'

And I'm startled because he didn't hear that it wasn't me. He didn't suspect for a moment that those words were not his wife's.

* * *

'Olivia is—'

Here we go. 'Don't you ever get sick of saying her name?'

'What?'

'The name "Olivia". You just seem to say it all the time now. I mean, *a lot.*'

'Beth, don't.'

I can't stop even though I know I shouldn't have started. I can hear the wickedness licking the sides of the words as they come out of my mouth. 'Life goes on, Steve. You know. We still have to buy milk and put the bins out. No matter how many children it might turn out you have.'

Steve laughs, but there's no mirth in it. 'I have three children. And one wife. That's it.'

'Well, your one wife is unhappy. And you don't even notice.'

'I notice.'

'But what? You don't care enough to do anything about it?'

I know he cares. He just doesn't know what to do so he is navigating life on its surface. No delving, staying on top where the skin forms. So I am swiping at him, trying to drag him under.

'I don't want you to be unhappy, Beth. And I don't want Jane in the way you think. She is my daughter's mother. That's all.'

His words scratch me like a briar. *My daughter's mother.* Isn't that me?

'But you have this option now. Another family, another

path to take when you tire of this one. Or even if you don't, I'll always feel like you might.' My grandmother's voice suddenly sings in my ears: *It doesn't do for a man to have options. Stops him focusing.* 'I have to coax you to participate in anything to do with Al and Mae, these days, but you're all go for Olivia.'

'Bring her in among us, then! That's what I want. She doesn't have to be outside us. Bring her in among us, and let's do things together. Please.' He is in full-on dreamer mode. He takes my hand. 'Someone else to be there for Mae, another girl. Can you just let us all be together? Just let us *be?*'

'If we bring her in, into what you call *us,* things won't, they won't – *hold,* Steve. The balance we have will be gone, and we will all lose.' My voice drops, draining down through me. 'Why can't she *just be* in England, and maybe she could visit us from time to time as she gets older? The odd Christmas or something.'

He knows I don't want her around at all. He stands up, his face readying for combat. 'I want to know my daughter, Beth,' his voice is growing stern, 'and I will. And I really want more than anything to have my wife's support on this. So you need to decide if you're going to have a problem giving it.'

I say nothing but look straight at him, this spoiled man, who expects too much. This dreamer who will have the world.

* * *

Another child.

Another child I hadn't planned for.

Like I hadn't thirty years ago, when I was a teenager sitting in the reception area of a house in Ealing, waiting to be called, blurting out my real name and my address in Ireland, forgetting to cover my tracks as I'd been told. My boyfriend at my side, skinny and out of his depth, thinking he could care for a baby when he still had braces on his teeth, a belt with a notch his dad had cut in, and his mother at home in Dublin ironing his school uniform for Monday.

We brought souvenirs back from London to hide the fact that we'd spent the day in an abortion clinic. My mother whispering into my ear as I came through the front door, 'It's for the best, Beth.'

Another child I hadn't planned for.

Like I hadn't planned for Mae.

'Is this what happens?' I say to Claire. 'Punishment throughout my life for the child I chose not to have? For what I did as a seventeen-year-old?'

'Christ, Beth! Is that what you think? That you're being punished by some Higher Power?'

'Well, I seem to be coming down with children. They're everywhere, Claire. Seriously. And they're not your average ones – they're *complicated*. Ones that aren't even bloody mine now. And Mae will be a child for life, really.'

'Yes, but you adore Mae. And she you. She is a wonder.'

'I know.'

'But this one,' Claire shakes her head, 'this one is Steve's problem.'

'Yes, but Steve is my problem.'

'You're not wrong there.'

'I just wish I could feel some kind of warmth, or benign acceptance, towards her. What's wrong with me? She's just a little girl. A beautiful little girl. None of this is her doing. She could as easily have been my child.' The familiar set of her brown eyes, the thick waves of dark hair. Surges of jealousy and guilt and nausea. 'But it seems the best I can hope for is to feel nothing at all.'

'I wish I could feel something benign about Steve at the moment, if I'm being honest,' Claire says.

'Did I give him too much freedom, do you think? A freedom that veered into neglect?' I ask us both. 'Is that what it was? Did a vacancy grow because I was caught up in Mae at the time? You know, because there wasn't enough weight from me, enough of a hold, to keep him at my side. Maybe Steve had freedoms then that he didn't know how to manage.'

Claire listens while I speak, listens to me unravel.

'I mean,' my voice is worn-out now, plaintive, 'why did he do it?'

'Because he wanted to.'

* * *

Our bell rings. I open the door and see Jane.

'I can't come in – my engine is running.'

'Oh. Okay. What can I—' I'm confused. 'Sorry – why is your engine running?'

'I left it on. Is Steve here?' she asks me, breezy. Hoping I won't get into it. After all, the engine's running.

'No.'

'Oh. I thought he would be. I'll go, then. Thanks.'

Fuck off.

* * *

I get Jane. I get her. I got her on sight. I knew what she was. Smiling and bright but always watchful. A restlessness about her, which is all ambition. The desire to get on, to climb the ladder – all the ladders – burns from her, livid like a flame. Nothing she has done since that first day in my kitchen has been at odds with what I saw in her then. And I don't expect it ever will. I don't expect she will ever surprise me, now that I know her better. I still get her. I was right.

And, of course, Claire is right too. Steve slept with her because he wanted to.

* * *

Mae and Olivia are pushing past each other, laughing, each trying to get out the door first. Half-sisters. Which half? I never had a sister, either a half or a whole one.

I wonder if they can feel it, a connection. Half a connection? Sharing lifeblood as they do.

* * *

He comes in.

He speaks and I speak. We are courteous, we eat together politely.

I make ordinary sounds and, over the evening, our eyes may meet for a second or two. Brief smiles. That's enough. Both of us are soft and defeated on our own side of the fence.

He puts out the recycling; I turn out the lights.

Most of love's power is how badly it hurts.

* * *

Have there been phone calls over the years? Words whispered upstairs, calls made from the bathroom? Too long spent in the car?

Have there been texts? Read and immediately deleted. Ping.

Replies read and deleted.

Backwards and forwards.

Ping, pong.

But, no. There can't have been. Or he'd have known about Olivia. And he didn't. I saw his stricken face that morning as he gripped the letter. When that post arrived just six weeks ago. A lifetime ago.

* * *

'Did you not put the washing on?'

He doesn't answer. We both know it wasn't a question.

I imagine I feel the ground in our bedroom shake as the cracks between us grow. The silences and misunderstandings have arrived here, left Vesey Hill, left Dublin, to invade this new place.

Doubt. Everything's in doubt. I look into the oval mirror and it's still me, all right. The Irish woman, the one who has the daughter with the disability. I'm more tanned, freckled, my hair a bit lighter than before. But it's me. And yet I feel completely at odds with myself, with my days and nights.

Part of me wants to throw myself at his feet, to grab his ankles and stop him moving, to make him laugh so we can love each other again, fully and simply. Right here in this room.

Jane knows it's independence that makes a woman desirable. Require nothing, be self-sufficient and fun and capable, and a man will move mountains to provide for you. To help. To give you what you don't even need. And then you can move on to getting whatever you actually want. It's a game and she has come to play.

By comparison I am dependent and sensitive to everything. Naked and ill-defined, a heap of feelings sludging through the day, either crying or shouting.

One night. And everything in ruins. And now a seemingly polite but most brutal assault on me, and on my family. Neither Mae nor I can compete. We both fall short in our categories. Jane and Olivia have us on conventional beauty, age and achievement.

Steve is behind me, taking off his suit. I see him reflected in the mirror, small in the background.

'I think I actually hate our life.'

He stops opening his shirt and stares at me.

It's a pointlessly alarming and sweeping thing for me to say, particularly as it's late and the day has been long and we're just about to get into bed. But I know I'm not going to be able to sleep, so I don't feel like he should find it so easy.

I can't believe I'm behaving this way at forty-eight years of age, and I tell myself that I'll be kinder in the morning, but there's a fire inside me right now, and there are words that need release.

'Please don't, Beth.' His voice is quiet. 'It's a really difficult time, I'll grant you that. But don't say you hate our life, what we have. I'm too tired for getting into this.'

He gets into bed. Keeps to his side.

'Steve, I spend my time looking at *our life, what we have.* Then I look at Jane's life and what she has. And what you have there. Then I think about money, how much of that we have, how much she will want, how much Mae will always need to live her life, and on and on and on, and every time I get bogged down in *what we have* and what we don't have, and in the real challenge of trying to find a silver lining.'

My words are tumbling out. They need space to move. 'How will we pay for this child?' I get into bed, keeping to my side. 'And – and how long will it be before you consider her mother again, if you haven't already?'

My darkest fear.

I turn off my lamp and lie still.

He plays dead.

They'll be gone in ten days, but I fear the jig is up even so. The last few years – the blissful time of our forgetting – is over.

* * *

Jane smiles and bestows. *Hello, shop girl. Hello, man walking by me on the street. Hello, Mae.* All white teeth and enunciation. She is the good fairy. *Come, come with me. What is it you desire?*

Around her, I grow quieter, more contained. Compressed. I am the black witch.

'*Sayonara,*' she had said, when she was leaving earlier, turning to look at Steve. '*Sayonara.*' She smiled. And her smile cut me out of the room.

And I knew she had said it to him before. Because he didn't question it and he didn't reply. He just gave a short cough and looked at me.

A warm acidic liquid has sat in my throat since. A vile ocean of things unsaid.

* * *

I watch him with Olivia, a man and his child. And I can see that that's how it appears, that that's what they are – just a hands-on dad and his beautiful daughter – if you were looking in from the outside. Like I am.

'I will always want you to love, actually to *prefer*, Al and Mae over Olivia,' I say later. 'That's the simple truth, Steve.'

'I can understand how you would,' he says, and nods, as though such a feeling from one's wife is reasonable.

I look at him, wondering if he hates me now.

* * *

Bill is sitting in his wheelchair, reaching up and carefully drying his dishes one by one – a cup, a saucer, a plate. His kitchen radio quietly tells of the tides and the sea-area forecast, and I wonder if living alone is really any lonelier than living as a pair. Everything is in its place here, everything honest. I can't imagine Bill ever having hurt another person, ever having chosen to deceive. The sun makes a triangle of light across the draining board, the room full of warmth and honour.

A nurse comes for a couple of hours every morning to do the things he can't. Before she leaves, she asks a few leading questions. It's his answers she's after, answers that might flag a decline, suggest another corner of him has stolen away overnight.

He still goes to Mass each day. He enjoys the familiarity, the routine of ceremony. I see nobility in this daily commitment and I envy it – his lifelong pledge to the Church, in sickness and in health.

'You have built a life together, and my son has risked it,' he says now. 'I love him with all of my heart but there are certainly weak edges to Steven. I know that. His mother adored him so much, Beth.' He looks up at me, his eyes always kind. 'Her only child. He was everything to her and she couldn't do enough for him, so I think his expectations of being loved might be rather high.' He smiles.

And the room is even warmer for having him in it.

'Ah, and she loved me well enough too, I suppose,' he says then, with a laugh, and reaches up to fill the kettle at the sink.

'I don't doubt it,' I say. 'The thing is, we don't really talk that much now, Steve and I. Things are either angry or silent. Mostly silent. I think I've become too sad for words.'

Bill nods. 'Silence can be golden, though. No need for all this talking about everything day and night, as is the fashion now. Think on it, Beth. How much damage has been done? Can you survive it? And do you want to? Those are the only questions.'

Before I leave, he squeezes my hand. 'You will survive this.'

* * *

Olivia and Jane are gaining ground. Pulling him apart, pulling him away. Us and Them. And Steve writhing on his hook in between. Survival.

How much damage has been done? And can you survive it? Do you want to? Bill's leading questions.

130

What are my answers, and do they flag a decline? Another corner of us having stolen away overnight.

Does Steve love me *well enough*?

You will survive this.

* * *

I look at my watch and imagine where you are for lunch. I listen to the radio reports and account for traffic so I can calculate when you should be home. Are you late because you're busy or is it because you linger?

I'm worn out.

Sometimes I think you're lovely.

There are things I could say but, if I started, who knows where I would stop or where it might end?

I am both reassured and unsettled by Steve's presence in the house now for exactly the same reason: it means he isn't somewhere else. It means he's here.

He stands up, fixes his tie, puts his jacket on, stacks the cup in the dishwasher, folds the newspaper under his arm, picks up his keys and wallet, and checks for his phone. Always checking for his phone.

Out the door.

So much movement. So little sound.

* * *

Stratum upon stratum, every look that passes between him and Jane, layer upon layer, every time I sigh at Olivia's name, small jibes and bigger hurts, layer upon layer, covering the rings made by the years gone before, pain on pain, pressing and reducing our past until it becomes something else, something altogether different.

Something hard and black.

Our bodies move around each other in the bathroom, careful not to brush a stray elbow or a moving hand. The air is condensed and heavy, and I think about opening the window. But it's better just to leave. There's no way around the hurt.

And yet it's familiar. This feeling is familiar. We have lived this way before. In this hard and black place that exists beneath the surface of love and wonderful things.

Those years ago, back in Dublin. Back when we were lost to each other and Steve met Jane for the first time. I recognise this heaviness. I feel it again.

Jane was at the beginning of what it turns out was now our end, and she's here for the final act and curtain. A dramatic integrity to it all. My life playing out, while I watch from the front row.

* * *

We speak through Mae.

'Mummy's busy being in charge of everything.'

'Daddy is tired again so we'll just go and have fun ourselves, darling.'

When our daughter's not at home and there is time to

talk, we don't. We have neither the language for it nor the energy.

* * *

'I actually nearly ran, Mum.' Al is animated, describing the kitchen scene this afternoon. 'I nearly ran out of the house. *Our* house. It felt so strange, so *wrong*, seeing Dad and her there, where you should be. I know they were just talking, and they have to talk, it's best for Olivia, I suppose, that they do – but still, I can't handle it. So I left, off down the garden, as if I was the intruder.'

He closes his eyes and squeezes the bridge of his nose. Just like his father.

'I still can't make sense of it. You know? In my head? I get the nuts and bolts of it, obviously, but I can't actually *understand* it. It's like this whole other weird world exists. Like playing one of those Xbox games where you haven't unlocked that part of the city yet so when you run at it you're bounced back by an invisible wall. You can't access what's in there. You can see it, but not as clearly – that world just won't light up for you. Won't let you make sense of it.'

I know exactly. An invisible wall.

'*And* she was wearing bloody linen trousers, for no good reason. White ones. I haven't seen a pair of those since we lived in Vesey Hill.'

I'm relieved to hear a bolt of humour through his

clouds. 'Well, now, tell me what would be a *good reason* for wearing linen trousers?'

'There isn't one. They look ridiculous, scream school gates, and crease like fuck.'

'Al—'

'Sorry. Crease *easily*. Also, they never fit properly.' He looks away for a moment, then smiles at me. A moment passes before he speaks quietly, 'how are you, though, Mum?' Nineteen years old and on fire, but still able to feel for me. 'How are you?', he asks again.

'I'm okay, honey.' I give his shoulder a gentle squeeze.

'Seriously, though. I don't understand Dad at all. Look at you – you're cool and smart and fun.' His voice cracks, but he continues: 'And then her – with the cheerleader hair and the stupid glamour.'

'It wasn't ever really anything to do with her, Al.' I breathe in. Give myself a moment before saying anything more. He watches me; he waits. 'To be fair to her, it was about your dad and me, at that time, and difficulties we were having in our marriage.'

'But after everything you guys have come through . . .'

'Well, maybe that's a little of why.'

He's frowning, but still listening.

'You're right. We did survive a fair bit of stuff. But a lot of it wasn't fun, you know. And for quite a while, it was hard. Hard for me, and for your dad.'

'I get that. I do. But why couldn't he buy a fancy car or

something? Not present us with this little girl – a little girl who looks just like a mini version of me.'

'Honestly, Al. He and I both made mistakes. Over a lifetime, people will break promises they meant to keep. Your dad did something stupid and selfish, but he wouldn't ever have meant to hurt us. And his bad decision has cost him dearly. The fact that he has let you down is unbearable for him. And he most certainly didn't want another baby – I can assure you of that.' I smile at my son, this man. 'It's really not about Jane, about him choosing her over me. It was just nothing, a mistake. He didn't have feelings for her then and he doesn't now.' I wish I was as convinced as I was managing to sound. 'But, you know, if you want to hate her discreetly, I'm okay with that.'

He smiles. 'I promise to.'

'Thanks.'

'And Olivia?'

'Olivia is just a child,' I say, looking at him.

'I know.' His voice is quiet. 'She hasn't done anything wrong.' He nods as he speaks.

'I should be nicer to her,' I say, realising suddenly that this is the simple truth.

* * *

We have come out in public to ignore each other. Just to break the monotony of doing it at home. Out into the open, where we must dress better for it. Important to keep the misery alive.

Steve sets his stool back from the bar. Now he can see past me, look around the room. I watch a couple to the left of us tilt their foreheads together, gentle. I turn away. The girl behind the bar raises her eyebrows at Steve. He nods and points at his glass.

I was ready early. I wanted to be the one to set the tone. I dressed up, so he'd feel he had to. I thought that maybe if we made an effort, if we looked good, we might feel it. Or we might behave better. That the effort might carry over into the rest of the evening.

It hasn't.

We're overdressed and drinking in silence.

Time drags itself along, minutes grinding out minutes. Everything is insufferable – the damp beer mats, the mostly empty wooden tables, the lines of upturned glasses warm and wet from the steaming dishwasher, the muted golf on the television in the corner. I get up and excuse myself.

No reaction.

The strip lights in the basement toilets make things ugly. Yellow and hollow, morgue-like. Tiled walls. Easier to wipe down. I look like death.

The stalls are all empty.

'Fuck,' I say to the mirror, half expecting the word to echo.

The door opens and I resent the intrusion.

It's him.

'Fucking hell, Steve. What are you doing in here?'

'I don't know. You just seemed to be a while and I – I'm cracking up just sitting there, staring at the clock. I want to go. I just want us to go home. You and me. Just go and be us at home. Why can't we do that? Why is it so fucking hard to just do that?' He bangs the tiled wall with the flat of his hand.

'Because I can't pretend that it doesn't matter. It's become all there is – everywhere I turn. You have this woman and you have a daughter, and they're both fucking perfect.'

Steve moves and sets off the hand-dryer. 'What can I do? Tell me what I can do. I'm just – I have another child, yes, but everything doesn't have to be ruined because of it. Because of a child. Surely.' He slides down the clammy wall and sits hunkered, his head in his hands.

A girl who looks like you, can talk to you, will grow with you, in ways that Mae never will. A girl you have been putting first.

'Another little girl can't feel all bad, Beth?' His voice is low – he's speaking towards the floor.

'But she's your girl, not mine. So it can feel totally shit to me.'

He looks up. 'Yes, she is my—'

'I swear, Steve, if you say, "She is my daughter," once more as long as we live I'll lose my mind. I KNOW! EVERYBODY KNOWS! You have two daughters now. There isn't a soul around who hasn't heard about Steve Rogers and his ready-made daughter. And how much she looks like him. What's it like, Steve, having a perfect daughter, smiling up at you like you're God Almighty?'

The air crackles between us, in this hollow, yellowed room, waiting for one of us to ignite it and finally set fire to ourselves, to each other, to the life we've built, once and for all.

I am whipped-up anger and ugly, jealous words. I can feel my pulse quickening, sweat prickling my armpits. I put my hand to the wall to stop the floor falling away. 'What are you going to do, Steve? What are you going to fucking do?' I badger him, tired of waiting. Tired of sulking on the fence. 'Because there seems to be no "we" about it any more. Clearly, you're going to call it. You're going to decide what happens next. So call it.'

He holds up his hand, signalling me to stop, to stop talking.

I stop. I will wait this out, here and now. In the murk of this pub toilet. I will wait until he is clear. Until he takes out his colours and chooses a mast.

'Beth, I – I love her. I know it's weird and I can't explain it, but I just do. I feel it.'

'You'd fucking better be talking about Olivia.'

'Of course I'm talking about Olivia! Jesus Christ!' He runs his hands through his hair. 'I love her. And what can I do about it? What would you have me do? It doesn't mean I love Mae, or you, or Al any less. Surely there's room for me to love you all.' He keeps going, all the time watching my face, reading my silence. 'She is Mae's half-sister,

Bethy. Maybe in the future, when we're older, we'll be glad of her. Strength in numbers and all that. It wouldn't just be Al, you know, responsible for Mae on his own. For the rest of his life. This girl, a part of Mae. Can you ever see that? A girl – a woman then – part of Mae's family, to help look out for her . . .'

His eyes are wet and I can see he means every word. He wants me to be happy that he has another child, that Mae might have a carer on the other side of the world in the far-distant future.

'Difficult and shitty things happen, Beth. They do. And I know you see this as one of them. As a shitty thing. But do you know what else happens? Love. Love happens. And it has. I love that little girl. Maybe you will someday too.'

He waits.

I say nothing. *Love happens.* Such a simple phrase, so lovely. So at odds with this basement morgue-toilet.

'I really need to be nearer to her. And this country, New Zealand, it's just too far away. Too far from England.' He breathes deeply. In and out.

I can hear my heartbeat in my ears, the bleed of a migraine starting to darken my mind.

'But I think Ireland makes sense.' He nods as he says it, tries to sound matter-of-fact, reasonable. Problem solved. 'I think we should go back. Everyone could be happy then.' Still nodding to his own words. 'You get to go home. Be among your family, your old friends. And the children too – they'll have their grandparents again. All of us together, you know? Back in Dublin. And I'll be nearer England. I can come and go a bit. This way, Olivia, well, everyone wins,' he says, his eyes looking away from mine.

I lean against the wall, nausea moving through me in waves, my mind all out of light now. Shock, maybe.

'You're always saying New Zealand is so far from things,' he goes on, using my words against me. 'Well, now you can go back, back to Europe. All of us will. Would you consider it, Bethy? Do you think you could imagine it?'

Relying on the wall to hold me, to keep the room in its shape.

'Can you hear me? I need us to go back. So everyone can be close.'

I am silent.

'Beth, can you hear me? What do you think?'

I can hear. What use is it what I think?

* * *

Shock. This migraine, this darkness.

Devastation. That's what it is.

* * *

Steve uses his fingers to count out how many days there are until Jane and Olivia leave.

Seven, I want to say. *For God's sake, it's seven.*

It's been less than two months since Jane's letter

arrived and in that time they've cast a net over our three years in New Zealand. A little girl has pulled everything into a pile – our memories, our closeness – and dragged it away beyond our reach. And I've no power to heave it back. Olivia has pulled our life to her, put herself at its centre, and will leave soon, hauling it behind her.

And it seems Steve would have us all go too: where she goes we must follow. Back. The four of us, the Rogers family of Auckland.

The Rogers family of Dublin.

Will she be a Rogers soon? Will she also take our very name?

But she is just a child, so I must be kind. She doesn't know her own strength.

And I didn't know the depths of our weakness.

* * *

'We can't seem to get along, to be happy together any more, Steve. And I don't think that moving anywhere – much less moving *back* – is going to change that.'

I know now that I've been wrong about our marriage. I've been wrong to think that we repaired it, then moved across the world – our love restored, intact – for warmth and freedom. All we did was up and move. We put land and sea between us and our past, but it has found us. Here, in the furthest corner of the world, in a different time zone, hiding among the sailboats.

We have been found out. Here in our hiding place, pretending.

'I'm not *un*happy. It's just different now. We could be happy again.' His voice is matter of fact. 'Yes. We will adapt and things will adjust.'

'You mean that *I* will adjust. That the children and I will haul our asses to the other side of the world, again, for you. And it will be about you, so of course you'll be happy.'

'Well, we're adults and surely we can work—'

'Sorry to stop you again, Steve, now you have everything so tidily organised in your mind, but when you say, "we're adults", I'm just clarifying that you mean you, me and Jane.'

'Yes. I do.' He nods. Definite.

'I can't.' I sigh. 'You see, Steve. *That*. How can you expect me to live with "we" now meaning *we three*?'

'Jesus, Beth. I don't even know what your problem *is*, half the time.' He walks towards the front door. 'But I can assure you that I AM FUCKING HAPPY, OKAY?' he roars over his shoulder.

A few minutes later my phone beeps: *I'm sorry. I love you x*

I'm sorry I love you too.

* * *

Mae, our emotional barometer, feels the tension in the house. 'You okay, Mama?'

'I'm okay, honey.'

She frowns and leaves the room. What would she say in these moments if her vocabulary matched her sensitivity?

She comes back with her soft bear. 'Teddy will mind you.'

* * *

I drop my bag on the kitchen table and walk quickly down the hall. 'Steve? Are you here?'

The house is empty.

The clock says just after seven p.m. But it feels later. Everything is darker.

He is out on the back porch reading and tapping the top of a pen on his closed teeth. I stand there. *Tap tap tap tap.* Pen on teeth.

I am at the kitchen table going through the post when he eventually comes in, moving through the room in an obnoxious way – touching things, lifting things, shrugging them off, putting them back askew, everything in this house suddenly foreign to him, out to get him. He moves around, watchful, noisy but not caring.

* * *

I meet with Mae's teacher, I do my work, I sweep the driveway, I read a poem, I go to the supermarket, I take a walk with Al, I remember to smile. I won't go down under this.

Steve turns away from me in bed, deliberately heaving

onto his side, lumbering to make sure I notice. As if I need any more clues. As if I don't know what I have to say, what I must agree to, where I need to go, to turn him back to me.

* * *

'Come on! Hurry up!' He slams his car door and the engine starts with a roar. His foot pointlessly agitates the accelerator.

I get in quickly.

The radio starts up and the car fills with some kind of dance track, a techno sound that Steve would call 'noise'. I look at the screen and see that someone has re-set his channel. Someone younger than either of us.

* * *

He batters me with heavy fists of silence now. He lifts his newspaper a little higher when I come into the room. His mood is sealed and he has pulled a boulder across. Control.

Your move, Beth.

I am to be the one to put the work in, to coax him back to me, to warm him up and win him back. I have been here before. In another place, when Mae was a baby and the weather was cold.

I make no move.

Stay cold, Steve. If that's what you want.

* * *

'Do you love him?' Claire's voice is clear.

'Yes.' Mine is equally clear. 'But I might hate him too.' I feel sad and dark, compacted like a stone.

Georgia and Mae are playing in the sand nearby. Separately. They are both building castles – one each.

'You have to decide whether you're all going back to Ireland, or not. I don't know what else to say to you, Beth. I suppose it comes down to what you want. Do you want to go back home? And what will happen if you do? What will happen to your family if you stay?'

I don't know.

I look at Mae, playing alone. She has enough stacked against her already.

* * *

He is in the garden, on the phone. He has covered his left ear with his hand to block out his surroundings. He is speaking. I am in the kitchen and can't make out any of his words. Then he stops and is listening. A smile curls his lips, a little laugh now, and then he is speaking again. Still smiling.

He looks down and kicks at nothing, rubbing the top of his shoe on the ground.

My stomach is leaden. The sun makes an oblong along the floor, joining up the kitchen tiles.

He finishes the call, puts his phone back in his pocket. Still smiling.

Watching him in these private moments, the slammed

doors open and the curtains part for me, and I see. Our domestic drama playing itself out.

I see.

He looks up, smiling broadly. Thinking over the call.

And then he sees.

He sees me. He stops smiling.

* * *

'I want it back, Mum. My family. You know?' Al's voice is low. 'Just the – the normal, boring security of it. Mum, dad, brother, sister. The certainty of us four. I don't want more people, or strength in numbers, or whatever.'

I hear Steve's phrase, *strength in numbers*. He wants us both to see it that way. I can't either.

'I don't want life experience or colour or whatever perspective I'm supposed to gain from all of this. I just want you and Dad, Mae and me. That's what I want.'

Me too.

'And maybe nineteen is too old to feel this way, and it's naïve or childish or something, but I do. Anything else just – it just hurts.' He sighs, rubs at his eyes. 'Not having Dad, like we did before. It's all just tangled up now. You know? I can't find the beginning or the end. It really hurts sometimes.'

It does.

* * *

Trying to warm to Olivia feels like trying to shout under water. It takes too much out of me and it's going nowhere.

'We have survived this long and this far, Steve. But we can't do this, this whole . . . *thing*.' I make a big circle with my arms. 'With Mae. And Al. And Olivia. It's just a mess. I feel like I can't – I just can't *be*. Your head is full of them, where once it was Mae and Al and me. Your family.'

'You are still—'

'Stop, Steve. Please. You can't feel what I feel. They're both your daughters. You want them both to be all they can. I don't. I want Olivia to be less great at school, and not the most popular girl in the room, and less perfect at ballet, and I want her not to look so like you. I actually think I want *the opposite* of everything you want for her. And I'm sorry about that. I really am.'

I am sorry. Sorry that I can't feel differently, sorry for my ugly feelings.

'So you'd be able to like Olivia if she was crap at things?' His tone is level.

'Honestly, I don't know. Probably. Maybe not. But I just hate – I'm just struggling with – the fact that she is better than Mae at absolutely everything. That she can do anything, but Mae can't.' My voice drops. 'I suppose that's what I mean.'

Steve looks right at me, his eyes wide. 'You'd prefer Olivia to be less able? Seriously, Beth, is that what you're saying?'

'No. Actually, I don't know. I think that maybe what I'm

147

saying is I'd find her easier to accept if Mae was more able. If she had fewer challenges.'

I don't look at his face because I'm uncomfortable now. Ashamed of my thoughts.

And I don't want to remember that I may still love him, damaged though we are.

'If Mae didn't have Down syndrome,' he says.

I stare at the floor.

'So you think that this can't work, that our family is finished, because our daughter has a disability which makes it difficult for you to cope with my non-disabled daughter?' He is almost laughing now and cruelty has crept into his words. 'So, if Mae was "normal", we would be happy? Or – even better, how about this? – if *Olivia* was the one with the disability, then it would be okay? You could allow her into my life then? If Olivia had Down syndrome and Mae didn't, the situation would be acceptable to you?'

And there it was. The worst truth. He had stumbled right into it.

'Is that it? Honestly, Beth! What the fuck?'

It sounded so shocking out loud, even to me.

My head swims. I don't know what I think now. I am the one with the problem. Am I? Is it me?

'So you're prepared to walk away? That's what you want?'

'I think it's reasonable for me to be completely *unprepared* for dealing with all of this, Steve,' I say quietly. I may be losing my mind, but I do know that. Warped as I have become, I still know that nothing could have prepared me for the mountain of crap that seems to be stuck to my plate. 'And I do have the right to struggle with jealousy – you must allow me that. To struggle with fear and insecurity. And with the destruction of the beautiful life I thought was ours. The idea of moving back to Ireland – it feels very much like moving *backwards*.' I breathe in, close my eyes to all of it. 'Giving up everything here – the friends I've made, the freedoms I have, the supports for Mae, our lifestyle as a family. And when I think about the upset this will cause our son, building his own life now, this moving back . . .'

And then I'm crying. Crying and talking, and not caring what I say any more because it's too late. And the worst of it has already been said.

'You are putting your new daughter first, ahead of our children.' My words are juddering along, tears streaking down my face. 'And it's really hard to take. To accept that I must go. Be a passenger in my own life. My children and I have to start again.'

'You won't be starting again – you're going home!'

'I left that *home* to create a new one, which I have to leave now, so that you can have it all.'

'You think that if we move back I will have it all?' he says. He shakes his head and walks out of the room.

'You'll have more than I will,' I shout at nobody.

* * *

When I sense Steve looking at me over breakfast, I refill my tea, then ask Al if he needs a lift and has enough money for the day.

It goes quiet again. The only sound is Steve's spoon stirring in his cup.

When it's time for him to leave for work, I look at the clock and then at him – for the first time since the evening before. My eyes are swollen from upset and lack of sleep. He appears his usual self.

He rises out of his chair and stands there, waiting. I'm not sure what he is expecting.

Al stands up. 'I'll walk out with you, Dad.'

I look at my son and smile. Grateful to him for backing us both, for keeping the ball rolling.

* * *

I turn our bedroom upside-down, upturn every drawer and box, looking for a letter or a payment or a bank statement or anything that suggests – what? Anything. Something.

I'm imagining baby-scan photos and clay imprints of Olivia's newborn feet. Imagining a set-up, Steve and Jane in on it together. A long-planned move back to Ireland so he can be near all of his girls.

I will prove that it wasn't a one-off. That it had been an affair. That there have been payments or arrangements or meetings of some kind.

I look for clues among the confusion of old car-insurance receipts and electricity bills.

I'm looking for a way out. A reason not to do the right thing.

I find nothing.

I have a glass of wine while I put everything away, before leaving to collect Mae from school. I glance in the rear-view mirror as I pull away from our street and see my hair is unruly and my lips are Merlot-stained. I'm mad about him. Mad.

* * *

Questions, questions, questions.

'Why can't Olivia be a priority? She's missed out until now. She's had none of me.'

'Don't you think that I should be with you, Al and Mae, and able to see Olivia too?'

'Don't you think that's what's best for everyone?'

'Don't you want to be nearer your parents as they get older?'

'Why must everything always be about how it makes *you* feel?'

Pressing, pressing. Pressure.

He starts to ask something else but all I can hear is the sound of my hairbrush as it makes lines through my hair. I stop when I see that his mouth is no longer moving.

He sighs, throws his hands into the air.

* * *

The cold shoulder, the looking away, the things we do in relationships to convey a message. *You have hurt my feelings. Please be kind. Please notice me.* It can be quite sweet, really, sometimes. In its gentleness and its need.

But this is something different.

We are in unknown territory now with a new sort of distance opening between us. This cold shoulder, this looking away. I can see no sweetness here, no bridge across it. Mae bound us in some indissoluble way. But Olivia has separated us in a similar way. And, of course, she is better at everything.

* * *

He texts me later. I see his name on my screen, a new message. Words are more reliable when they've been considered first, then typed, then sent. As I click on it, I feel a small surge of hope. But then I read, *This can't go on.*

I wonder how long he spent arranging those four words. Getting the tone right. Or if he just punched the letters in because he keeps his considered responses for someone else now.

It is early evening and not even a hair's breadth divides the sky and sea. I stand at the water's edge watching sailboats rise and fall, adapting to what's around them. Going with the flow, as they must, these small boats in the big sea.

When I walk into the kitchen, Steve is standing with his back to me. He is looking out the window towards the street I just came up. He would have seen me coming. The only movement he makes, knowing I'm behind him and within touching distance, is the folding of his arms.

I decide not to tell him right now, not to tell him that I have had a little time to consider it and that we will go. We will all go back to Dublin. So that a girl can know her father. As all girls should.

* * *

Al and I sit out on the lawn under the pohutukawa tree. I've been half expecting it to collapse or to burst into flames lately, to destroy itself somehow out of horror. But it stands solid. Ever ready to shelter a family.

'We'll see how it goes, Mum. You know, how things go with you and Dad. And all that. Maybe you'll be back here. Maybe it'll be sooner than you think.' He gives me a small smile. 'The rain might get the better of you guys. But,' he looks directly at me now, 'it's better for me to stay.'

Despite the pain slicing through my chest, and despite the mess we have made of things for him, I can hear that he has confidence in the decision he's made. That these are not just words, that he does want to stay. And that he will. I hope his confidence won't desert him when we do.

'I'd rather be here with you, honey,' I say, and hug him to me.

It's true, even though it might be disloyal to Steve for me to say it. What about my loyalty to my son? To this

153

man in front of me. What are the rules there? What are the ties? Are there none because he is over a certain age? Maybe he's not mine at all any more.

Fuck that.

I pull back and hold his face in my hands. 'You know I'd rather stay if we could somehow, so I could be with you?' Tears sit pooled in his eyes. This young man, my beautiful son.

And I hope he doesn't feel what I do now, the cold wind of loss already coiling around me.

'I know, Mum. But I need to grow up, do things for myself. I'll be fine. I'm actually looking forward to living on campus. I really am. And I'll have Papa Bill to stay with whenever I want. And you know that Lisa's parents will keep an eye too, no doubt. We'll Skype all the time, you and I. Every day. And Mae.' He gives a toss of his head, shaking off feelings.

I nod. 'And I'll always be there for you,' I say to the boy I'm leaving half a world away.

We look towards the house, its porch and the giant swing. It's pretty much the same as it was on that warm December day when we first saw it, but now it feels wrong. Let down. As though a dark secret has pushed its way from within the walls and assaulted us all. No more playing pretend.

I want to stand in front of Al, to shield him from the world. But I see that the world isn't the source of his problems. We are, and we need to get out of his way. He is ready for life without our chaos, without having to step over our mess every day.

He will be free, I tell myself.

Independent, I tell myself.

It will be the making of him, I tell myself.

It's not for ever, I tell myself.

He is ready for university here, ready to make art, ready to make his way, I tell myself.

Maybe he'll create something positive out of the knots and snags we have bequeathed him. I imagine seeing them on a gallery wall in the future. Scars framed, on show. *Collapse & Abandonment*, in watercolour. Christ.

'Do you think you and Dad will get a divorce?' Al pulls at a button on his shirt, checking the stitching, aware of himself and the weight of his question.

'I really don't know, honey.'

'It just makes me so sad when I think about him caring for someone else the way he does about us.' The rims of his eyes are red. 'And then I don't know if that's just selfish of me. But I can't – it still just doesn't seem right,' he says.

It really doesn't.

'It's shit, Mum. For you, I mean.'

'Yeah, it is. But, you know, Al, he's still Dad and he loves us just as much as before any of us knew about Olivia. And I feel the same too. Love is a strange thing – it's sturdy and fragile all at once.'

'But you'll probably end up getting divorced?'

'Well, the reality is that a feeling, however strong it may

be, can't flatten every day-to-day obstacle. Unfortunately. It can't smooth over every jagged edge. This little girl and her mother, where they live and all that, well, it's a bloody big obstacle, so while I do still love your father – and I always will – I'm finding it hard to maintain my sense of things as they were before. Trust and commitment. Your dad and I as one team. Making decisions together. Can you understand that?'

'Totally. Too many tangles.' He sighs.

And I feel it in that moment, the understanding that exists between him and me. And then I wonder if Steve and Olivia might grow to have such a bond. And I know that I shouldn't stand in their way. That I can't. I can't stand between a parent and a child.

'I'm finding it really difficult to get over Olivia.' I startle myself, speaking these words aloud.

'For you? Or for Mae?' Al. My lovely, gentle Al. Getting it, seeing it, seeing me. Mae is something I carry inside me, outside me, and always will.

'It feels like they're the same thing, really. She reminds me of too much. I can't seem to let her in. And it's foolish of me – actually, it's worse than that. It's unkind. She's an innocent little girl. Like any other. Like Mae is.'

He nods. 'Does he get it? You know, does Dad *get* how much hurt he's caused?'

'I think so.' *I don't know if he can.*

We are quiet for a while.

'It'll be good that I'm here anyway,' he says then, before

the silence beds in. 'For Papa. I'll be able to call in to see him every week. There's plenty of him left, you know.' He taps the side of his temple. 'Plenty still going on up here.'

I smile. We both know that most of Bill has left, moved on. The vital parts of his mind, the parts that made him who he was, have been creeping out the back door for some time.

'Fucking love,' Al says now, his voice a whisper. 'I'd sooner run headlong into a wall.' He starts pulling at his shoelace. 'You know, Mum, when I paint – this is going to sound really corny but when I paint, everything seems less of a mess. I mean it's the same mess, the same stuff, but it's as though I can paint my way through it. I can get it out, paint it out of me. Onto a page or a canvas or wherever.'

He looks up at me and smiles, and his face is a wonder. And pain soaks through me, like dye. I know that the stain, the mark of leaving him behind, will never come out.

That night I look into his room and see him sitting on the bed going through his paintings, his long tanned legs splayed in front of him. He is so young. He was born and raised in Ireland, but he is doing his growing up in New Zealand.

He's right: *fucking love.*

* * *

Mae pulls her little knees to her and straps her arms

around them. She can feel the shifting sands. I explain that we are going home to where we used to live to see Granny and Granddad, to stay there again. I show her a photo of them standing on the step outside their house. My childhood house. I say that we will see our old friends. But I struggle to think of any she will remember.

'And Al will come too?' she asks.

'No, Al will stay here for a while longer. But then he'll come. For a holiday! Or – even better! – we'll come back here to see him. It'll be exciting!' My words come out strangled and unconvincing.

Most children assume things are fine and normal until an adult tells them they're not. But Mae isn't like most children. Her eyes hold mine, looking for the truth, deciphering my real emotions, so she can decide how she really feels about this. About being separated from her brother.

* * *

Bill has had another stroke. Another piece of him has broken off and stolen away. I wonder how much of him can be left.

'It was shock that caused it,' Al says, through tears, and Steve and I let it go, put this opinion down to his upset. Pretend it's not the suspicion that thickens the air around us.

But he goes on, our son, not letting go: 'It's going to kill Papa Bill. What you've done.' He is facing his father, standing tall right in front of him. 'Olivia. And all that.' He waves a dismissive hand, brushing the idea of them away. 'You don't want to hear it, but it's true. You didn't see Papa wanting to meet her, or her mother. He couldn't bear it.' His face is streaked and puffy and his voice rages out of him. 'His loyalty is to Mae. And to me and Mum. He's better than you. He couldn't make sense of it and now he won't have to. Soon he won't be able to make sense of anything much ever again.'

He presses the heels of his hands into his eyes, breathes in.

'He knew.' His voice more controlled now. 'Papa *knew* you were going to leave, and that Mum and Mae would have to go too. He knew. But don't you worry about your plans, *Dad*. I'll stay with him. I'll be here for him, when you aren't.'

And then he is crying hard, crying for all of it, for his papa losing the struggle with his mind, and for his own losses, the loss of everything familiar.

'I'll take your place here. You're free to go.' My son is almost shouting now at his father. And my heart is crushed listening to it. I put my arms around him, my gorgeous boy, and he buckles onto me and sobs.

Steve closes his eyes, stands. There is nothing he can say.

* * *

The family is in freefall. People hitting every branch on their way down.

* * *

Steve rings from his father's house, where he is spending a couple of days.

I point at the receiver and widen my eyes at Al. *Do you want to speak to Dad?*

He shakes his head, shuts his sketch book and goes upstairs to his bedroom.

'He's not here at the moment, Steve,' I lie. 'You guys will work it out. Just give Al some time,' I say, despite knowing there is very little of that left.

Mae stands at my leg, her hand up, waiting politely, her eyes fixed on my face in case I should forget her. I pass her the phone and she gives a little fist pump before taking it, which makes me smile.

'Hi, Dad!'

I only hear her side of things.

'Me. It's me! Mae!'

'No! *Mae!*' She giggles. 'I played hockey at school today . . . Not horsey! *Hockey.*' She laughs. 'I'm too big for horsey. And we don't play that *at school!*' She looks at me, rolls her eyes dramatically. 'Yes, Al's here . . . He is here! I saw him . . . He went upstairs . . . Okay, I'll get Mama . . . I love you too. Mama, Dad wants you.' She passes me the phone.

'Okay, Steve, he is here,' I say. 'I'm sorry, but he doesn't want to talk to you right now. You've hurt him. And he's afraid you're going to do it again.'

I realise then that it's actually my son and me who are in the same boat.

* * *

His father's stroke doesn't change Steve's point of view. It blackens him further. He is put upon by this world.

Time is ticking. His daughter is leaving next week and his father is being lost to him too.

Nothing escapes his attention. He has something to say now, questions to raise, about everything. The things I do, the routines of our home. Everything an irritation.

'I don't know why you always leave the toast in so long. It tastes burned.'

'You need to keep stirring the eggs.'

'Why do you use that lifter on the pan? It scrapes it.'

'Why would you buy that dressing? The other one's much nicer.'

'I wish you wouldn't leave the landing light on overnight.'

'Don't park there. I don't know why you always park there.'

'Just leave it. You never manage it properly.'

Claire rings and asks how things are. 'It's a critical time,' I say.

* * *

'You're hanging off the cliff,' my father says, in a rare exchange between us. It is only him on Skype today. He has heard there is a crisis and sweeps in to manage it. 'This is the cliff.' His hand in a horizontal position fills my iPhone screen. 'Do you want to let go and set yourself free, or do you want to claw your way up off the edge and claim back what is yours?' I can hear his determination, his not-quitting.

He can't see that I'm already a dot falling to the ground, the cliff behind me.

In many ways, I'm not my father's daughter.

* * *

We sit in the garden, Steve and I. It's not so much that we're together, rather that we're both sitting outside at the same time.

To no longer be married. To be *un*married. To not be a wife.

For twenty years, I've felt our marriage as an actual physical thing, an invisible enclosure, containing me and holding me, for better or worse. Now I'm a mime, feeling along walls that aren't there, pushing against nothing, searching for a panel that moves. But something strong and unseen won't let me out.

Love.

And then his phone sounds, a text message. But he doesn't react. He ignores it, leaves it for later. I have stopped him looking, by being here in the garden too.

One by one the love lights are going out and we are losing all of our power.

Olivia is the fault line running her fingers through our lives, our marriage. Causing new cracks, and growing ones that are already there, barely patched over. She is an innocent, yet she has unsettled us, unearthed us irreparably. She is the line connecting Steve to Jane for ever.

She is our earthquake, small but violent.

An act of God.

* * *

Steve wakens during the night and sits up. He looks right at me, right through me. And then he lies down again.

I know this because I am awake, watching my life go into shut-down mode.

'Good night,' I say, reaching. And in the quiet gap, waiting for an answer, I finally fall asleep.

* * *

I'm calm when he isn't in the house. When he isn't due back. The man I knew has been replaced by something else, a bigger mass that takes up the room with giant overbearing silences and impatient remarks, while all the balls he's thrown into the air rain down on us.

I have stopped obsessing over the quiet, stopped looking for arrows and signposts between his angry lines.

I prefer it when he's gone.

His accent is starting to grate on me, every inflection and unfinished simile an annoyance. *Sweet as, big as, small as, hot as.* It's annoying as.

'Make sure you remember your phone,' I said, to his broad back, when he was leaving for work this morning.

163

He went still for a moment, then continued out the door without answering or looking around. Pissed off as.

Four days until they leave.

* * *

It would be safer, just the three of us – Al, Mae and me. We would move in step with each other. Six is too many. Too many women and children.

I look at the back of his head over the top of the couch. He is just one man.

* * *

Everything has been trampled on, nothing spared.

Steve and I each want the impossible – a happy-ever-after.

How smitten I was when we first met and how happy our life then. My hours spent either with him, or waiting to meet him. Sitting close in his Valiant with the single front seat, him gorgeous in low-rise jeans and layered tops.

I was twenty-four then and he was twenty-six. And I was different with him from the start – I didn't smile at other men, didn't mention it if they smiled at me. Something about him had changed everything. I wanted to protect him, to love him. To have his arms around me always, warm and solid. Potential stretched in front of us in every direction. We had all the choices and nothing but endless days to make them.

Our marriage is a broken bird now, caught in the wind too many times.

* * *

He is bent away from me, busy over the kitchen sink, digging mud from the grooves in his golf shoes.

'I booked the flights home – back – today,' I say.

His hands stop working, but he doesn't turn around.

'For all of us,' I go on. 'Well, for you and Mae and me.' Still nothing.

'Three one-way tickets,' I add pointlessly.

'Did you say it to Al?' His words, said quietly.

'Yes, before I rang to book them. He feels just as he did. His decision is still to stay.'

He blows out his cheeks. 'Well, I suppose it has to be his choice.' He starts to bang the soles of the golf shoes together and the noise, the slow clap of them, irritates me beyond reason.

'A choice he shouldn't have had to make, though, Steve,' I say. The clapping stops. I am speaking to the back of him, but even so I display my son's two choices using my hands. 'His parents and sister *or* his career here, his friends and his adult life.' I stand, arms out, invisible choices held aloft. 'Anyway, it was never any choice at all. This is his life, where we are now. Where he moved to three years ago, also because of you.'

He turns around, golf shoes for hands. 'So I'm a

dickhead and, because of that, our son is losing his family. That's the way you see it.'

I breathe in, try to see it a different way.

A row circles above us, all potential, curling and watching.

'Well, Al has to lose. And there's only one reason for that, only one reason he has to choose which loss to go for. And it's you, Steve. You're the reason.'

He turns back and slams the shoes onto the sideboard. He runs the tap on full and makes like he's going to wash the plates that are sitting in the sink. As though cleaning up was ever part of his plan. I watch him stack dishes smeared with food and mud spatters into a single pile. Too high. The hot tap is running. Too high. Water gushes out over the tower of crockery, bits of mud splash up. Spray the window sill. Spray his golf shoes. The mess he has made. Worse than before he started.

And I feel violence towards him, towards the chaos he causes. 'Mae has precious few people in her life who understand and love her like Al, and because of you, she is being separated from him. Her one sibling.'

With the last three words I dare him, the blackness rising in me.

Go on. I double-dare you.

'It doesn't have to be for ever, Beth. Jesus. It's not for life.' He turns off the taps, stands still.

'You're planning on out-growing Olivia?'

I feel the row curl down and wind around us now, like a snake.

He turns to me slowly. 'I meant' – a hiss licking his words – 'that Al won't be away from us, from you, for ever.' He brushes strands of hair back from his forehead where sweat is beading.

'And how do you know that?' An ugly snarl in my voice. 'He is starting his life as an adult and he is doing it here. On the other side of the world to Jane, Olivia and us.'

'We don't have any idea where Al's life will take him, Beth. And neither does he. Who knows where he'll end up? He talks about Europe all the time. Just let it be. Stop making such a big fucking deal out of it. He's European, and home is home in the end.'

'He's European?' I laugh. 'You've spent nineteen years telling him and anyone who'd listen that he's a Kiwi. But that doesn't suit you now, doesn't suit this bend in your road.'

'If we give him some time, I think he'll decide to follow us back.'

'Well, I'm pretty sure that our son won't be following our mess anywhere, anytime soon. So don't fool yourself.'

He walks out of the kitchen, leaving the muddy dishes stacked high for me.

* * *

Before Jane leaves to go back to London with Olivia, she and I meet alone, to talk. To clear the air. I was satisfied with murky air, but in a display of maturity I didn't feel, I'd agreed when Steve suggested it a week ago.

Presumably she agreed for Olivia, for the future. And probably to please Steve.

And I imagine neither of us wanted to appear less agreeable than the other.

'If you like good coffee,' he had spoken earnestly to Jane, while dropping a pin on her Google Maps, 'then that's the place you should meet.'

No, Steve, she likes crap coffee.

'Okay! I'll be there. Looking forward!'

I had to go. And, also, I was a bit curious to hear her side of the shit storm.

I arrive far too early. I stare at the door, pat down my hair, check my watch. And then I mess up my hair – I'm not here to impress her. To show her what Steve has at home.

I pick up the newspaper left on the table beside me. My eyes move across the print, taking in nothing. I put it back.

Just two days left. Just two more days until they leave.

I take a deep breath.

I tell myself that we're both here for our daughters, doing what's best for them. And maybe it'll be interesting to speak to her without my husband as a constant audience, our conduit. She might confirm how weak he is, maybe even throw up some further betrayal, the force of which would reduce our marriage to rubble, collapse it into an easy heap. Irreparable. I could dust off, walk away from him, resolved that it had been my only option. That everyone would say so.

I look around this place that Steve recommended. Upholstered old kitchen chairs, all painted different chalky colours. Brightly patterned wax tablecloths. Cute. Completely at odds with the conversation it's about to facilitate, its friendly pastels mocking my wood-stained mood.

Or perhaps it will go really well. Maybe in an hour we'll be laughing gaily at the whole beautiful mess of children and homes and continents. Ha-ha-ha. Chalky peaches and lemons all round.

No.

She comes through the door five minutes late. She's wearing jeans, boots with heels, and a tight grey marl vest top; a celebrity dressed down at the weekend.

And yet, even with all this, I can't say she's sexy. I've *got* her all along, and now that I know her better, I see there's peculiarly little about her that I'd call sexy. No heat beyond the surface. A beautiful face and a body for miles, yes, but her desire is to be whatever's required, her ambition to be a reflection. Big smile. No heat.

As we are two women meeting for coffee, we must observe certain norms. We must behave. Which means I can't give her a shove into the wall and run out the door. I can't stand on the table, point at her and tell everyone what I really think. I must join her at the counter, we must make choices, we must order, and someone must pay.

'I insist, Beth.'

'Okay so.'

There are things we do every day without thinking. But as I'm over-thinking myself into confusion, I drop my unopened wallet and leave my phone on the counter.

I return to the window seat I had chosen for myself. I must sit. Sit. And stay.

Jane sits down opposite me.

A milk jug, a tiny cauldron-shaped bowl of brown sugar, and a single flower in a short vase are all that divides us.

There is nothing more to be done now than raise our eyes to each other, two women thrown into each other's company by a man who's hoping we'll sweep his chaos into a corner for him and make everything nice, once and for all.

I take a deep breath, force my shoulders to drop on the exhale.

Jane's eyes are bright with what looks like a kind of amusement. The sunlight from the window behind me falls onto her face and chest, brightening her even further.

Still, though, no heat.

Her hair, her tiny pores, her mouth – her mouth. I shake my head to dislodge the thought.

After a moment, the waitress comes, carrying our drinks, and thanking her is the first thing either of us has said since we sat down.

I notice a man at another table looking at Jane's breasts. He sees me watching him and turns away. I'm the chastising older sister. He can't be bothered giving me a second glance.

I had entertained notions of speaking to the heart of her, with reason and maturity. Woman to woman.

'All this time, you were waiting in the long grass.'

Not the reasoned opener I'd rehearsed, but I was up and running. 'You knew. All these years, you knew you would come for him. And you found him – easily enough, I imagine – and you plotted, and you waited, and then you turned up on the other side of the world. Why? Why now?'

My heart has been taken by surprise, the rush of my own words catching it off guard. I feel its rapid beating, trying to escape my chest, like a child in a burning building.

Her voice is controlled and level when she answers me. 'Steve is a wonderful guy, Beth. A real gem.' She states this as a fact, despite knowing – actually *knowing BETTER THAN ANYONE* – that he has, among other deceits, cheated on his wife. 'A good man,' she goes on.

So definite is she that, suddenly and bizarrely, I wonder if she's wearing a wire.

'I know that,' I say. Just in case he's sitting in a van outside, listening.

'And I'm not trying to break up your marriage. I don't want your husband. I can't deny that I felt a connection with him, but what we— It was years ago.'

'*It* was during my marriage.'

'I know but, really, it won't ever come to anything. It's – it's nothing now.' Those were her words but her tone, her hesitation, suggested she felt more than nothing.

'So why are you here, then? Pursuing this nothing?'

'I understand that you are his wife, Beth, and that you have Mae, you have children with him—'

'And an entire life,' I cut across her.

'And a life, yes. But I also have a child with him, his youngest child and—'

'With respect, Jane, I didn't come here to compare stories with you. Or to justify my claim on my own family or on my husband of twenty years. Please let's not overstate who you are. A man, who had an awful lot on his plate at the time, had sex with you. Once.'

Her eyes widened and she straightened in her chair as I spoke. I hoped it was my candour she was reacting to.

And not that I was wrong about it being just the once.

'I can't imagine what it's been like for you, Beth. With Mae. And I don't want to make life harder for her.'

'Do you want to know what it's been like for me, with Mae?' I don't wait for a response. 'It's been great. The last few years have been just wonderful. We moved here as a family, and we had a life full of love and warm weather and the ocean and bare feet, the whole nine yards. All of us buoyed up. And Mae as happy as can be.'

She looks down at the table.

'And then you arrived. On our doorstep. In our lives. And now, now we're leaving everything. And our son is staying. You brought your past across the world and into my present. Into my family's future. So now we actually do have a problem with Mae. Because she is leaving what she knows, her friends, her school, her grandfather, and her brother, whom she adores. So don't waste your time imagining what my life has been like with Mae, but rather try to imagine what it's going to be like. She is facing into a whole new *everything*, and without Al. And then try to imagine what it will be like for my son, having his family leave him. You have most definitely made Mae's life harder. And Al's. And don't get me started on mine.'

The pressure has been building in my head all morning, in my chest. But, oh, now the sweet and vicious relief. Like a window opening. Or one of those fucking huge glass sliding doors they have everywhere in this country.

'I didn't know anything about his life, nothing much about the children, despite how much he spoke about you. About how he felt.'

I wince at the thought of Steve unburdening himself of his marital woes to a blonde stranger in a bar. Asshole.

'I see that even more so now,' she adds. 'That I knew nothing, really.'

'But you did know he was married.'

'Yes, and I'm sorry for that, but it should have mattered more to him than to me, surely.'

I look away and say nothing.

'I didn't know – I didn't know about Mae.' She leans forward in her chair, as though she's confiding in me. 'About her disability. I knew he had kids but I did want to say that to you today, if nothing else – I didn't know he had a child with Down syndrome.'

Families such as mine are to be pitied. Not threatened

and toppled with casual sex and frivolous encounters. I think she gives a small shiver. Or maybe it's me.

'So married men with run-of-the-mill children are fair game, but you'd consider drawing the line at the fathers of children with disabilities? Or do you mean that you'd still have done it but you'd have felt some regret afterwards? Or do you mean that you'd have still done it but you'd have made at least some effort not to get pregnant?'

I sound hysterical. I can hear myself losing it but I don't care. The dam has burst.

The man is staring again. I don't know if it's the breasts or my apparent madness that has him transfixed.

'You have compromised Mae's position with her brother and with her father. Your actions have done that,' I say piously.

'I see where you're coming from,' she says, her voice quiet.

A moment of silence passes between us.

'I have to say, though,' she's on the steady climb back already, 'I think you're focusing too much on me, on a power over your husband that I didn't have. I don't think he would have been so readily . . .' she pauses, choosing her words '. . . *available*, had he been happy.'

She looks down at her clasped fingers as though she is a demure and elegant thing, guilty of nothing but her obliging nature and her beauty, bravely shouldering their weight. Seeing her recover so quickly, hearing her pontificate about my husband's happiness after my unhinged rant, makes my hands shake. And what I hate most, sitting there trembling, with the manky old yellow rose on the table between us, is that I know she's right. Steve couldn't have been seduced unless he'd wanted to be.

'You arrived here to invade our lives.' Each of my words is sharp, their edges like knives. 'Lives you knew – and still know – nothing about. Steve was married and he lived with his wife and their two children. That much you were aware of, when you knocked on our door.'

'I know. But it felt important. I felt like I had no choice. Every child deserves to know their parents. And that means – whether you like it or not – that Olivia does too.'

I am silent.

Her eyes look to mine, and her voice loses its grit. 'I never knew my father, Beth.'

I stay silent, wait to see where this new guff is going.

'I've never met him. And that has left a mark on me, a sense of loss that I've always carried. That I still carry. And I really don't want that for my daughter. I can't bear that I actually did the same thing, that I grew up and had a child, and that she . . .' She straightens a bit in the chair, clears her throat. 'Beth, I just couldn't have Olivia not know her father either. I'm sorry.' Her eyes have filled with tears. 'I was desperate for Olivia to meet him, to meet Steve. Just to know who he is, to see that he's a nice guy, because even that's more than I ever had.'

I see a real dent in her. A dent in Jane, this beautiful younger woman who never knew her father. And I don't know what to feel, or how to react, but it stops me in my tracks. Because I believe her.

'I didn't mean to disrupt your family, what you have together. I really didn't. But children should know their fathers, Beth. I've thought about it every which way for years now, and each time it's come down to this for me. Daughters should know their fathers. I don't know what else I can say.'

'What will you tell her about how you and her father met? How will you explain me, Al and Mae?'

'I'll be honest with her. That's all I can do. And I hope that things between you and Steve will work themselves out. There's no reason why they shouldn't.' She pushes her chair back, readying herself to stand. 'I should go.'

'One thing I've been meaning to ask,' I say quickly. 'Why that photo?'

'Pardon?' She pulls herself, her chair, back into the table.

'Why did you send that photo of Olivia? One that needed cutting.'

'Oh, it was taken and printed specially, to post here. If that's what you mean. It wasn't an old one or anything. She's wearing her new princess dress in it. I cut the picture after. I changed my mind about it.'

'I presume it was you that was cut out of it?'

She nods. 'I thought it was best if this was just about Olivia.'

Well, it would never have made it onto the fridge if you

were in it is what I want to respond, but instead I just nod and hear myself say, 'That's what I assumed.'

I'm learning.

I stand up. I'll be the one to leave, not the one to be left. As though this is a game, and leaving first is the winning of it.

I'm not learning that much.

I edge out unsteadily from my side of the table and cross the floor, despite the feeling of vertigo that threatens to topple me. And then I pull the door too hard, as though Jane's decorum and her lovely daughter and her never knowing her father are the fault of the café with the good coffee.

* * *

One day left.

Olivia and Mae are standing on the beach, holding shells to each other's ears.

And I see it. I see that there is something lovely in the set of their bodies, in the way they are holding their heads close and whispering, conferring, giggling. I watch Olivia smile at Mae and reach out a reassuring little hand. Mae hesitates for a moment, then jumps over a sandcastle – clearing it easily. She glances behind her, sees the castle intact, and her smile is a beam. She takes Olivia's outstretched hand and looks at her as if she has all the answers.

They will probably know each other for a long time. Olivia will learn to read between lines that my daughter won't see, but I imagine they could be friends. And I know that if Olivia's good enough for Mae, she should really be good enough for me.

* * *

No more days.

I don't avert my eyes. I stand and watch. The three of them on our front lawn – Steve, Jane and Olivia. Their story will be endlessly retold – even I will have to tell it. So I need to get behind it, or in front of it, whichever means acceptance, that means damage limitation.

'Goodbye, for now,' Steve says to them.

Steve. I see him as a man, a man who is someone other than my husband. A man who can't navigate life all that well. A man who insisted on a paper map, guide book and two different iPhone apps on our weekend in Rome. As though there was anything but beauty and passion and drama every which way.

'Bye, Daddy.' Olivia's voice is like a punch in the stomach. *Daddy.*

He puts his hands under her arms and pulls her up along him – her white leather sandals dragging up his legs. In the past, I've watched him do that with Al and, until about a year ago, with Mae. But only Olivia is light enough now. And the whole movement – the lift, the eyes, the laugh – stirs up every barely controlled hurt. My head feels hot, full to the brim of warm, uncried tears. A huge branch rises out of him, stretched in another direction for as far as anyone can see.

Olivia will be fine. She will come to know her father, or a version of him, through her life. She'll probably come to know him better than I do. And I realise, standing there, that that's okay. Daughters should know their fathers.

And I think then that I will try better with my own. That I might phone him tonight, phone Dublin.

They go, Jane and Olivia. They disappear from view. They leave this lawn, this city, this country. And I am glad. A shot of relief dances through me. But it doesn't linger. My husband and I have lost each other to the fact of them, because there was already a crack between us that allowed too much pain in.

When Steve comes back up the steps my face is hot, streaked with tears and old love.

* * *

The house stands, stock still. Steve makes an effort – gives small smiles, nods when I speak. He hangs around a lot these evenings, waiting. Looking into the fridge, seeing nothing. Waiting. Opening doors and closing them. Waiting. Preparing himself for leaving. Displaced already.

The ghost of Olivia hangs in every corner.

I should have been better. Why couldn't I have been better while she was here?

I test myself by imagining her older, sitting on the tube on her way to study at Central Saint Martins or some other cool set-up. Her dark looks catch the eyes of other commuters, and all the choices in the world are hers.

And I find that my skin doesn't itch and my stomach doesn't turn.

I know that Mae will still think she's great. Because Mae's always been better than me at living – warm and open, she knows how to love more and to care less.

* * *

I lower myself onto the sand and we sit side by side, my husband and I. The sun dances on the water in front of us.

'The joy in being wanted, Beth. Do you remember that – the sheer *joy* of falling in love? And the hope of what might come.'

I do remember. The shiny, undamaged lure of new love.

There's been a lot of water under the bridge since we last felt like that. A lot of water, struggling to lift our sludge and move it along.

Our sludge. Our real, but unworkable, laden-down love. Damaged years ago. We'd managed to hide the rupture from each other, from ourselves. But now we know, and we must act on this knowing.

The situation in its quiet finality is lent some wonderful drama by the setting. The determined waves, the sky a mid-morning blue. We are a picture sitting here, one of those *Love is . . .* comic strips from the sixties, but for today's readers, for the world we live in now. *'Love is . . . sitting in the wreckage of your marriage.'*

On this summer's day, here on the sand, Steve and I come to an end. There is nothing left to hope for. I lean into him and the sides of our heads touch, delicately toasting our own demise.

And yet it is still light. Still early, not even noon. The accepted run of things is to continue without even a few hours of darkness to absorb this change. To register our dissolution. The afternoon will come soon and centre itself around our kitchen in its after-school way, as always.

The call of the birds, the giant trees with their canopies of clutched berries, the movement of the waves, the rise and fall of the boats . . . We stand up and leave them all to it, to this normal day.

Life. It goes on, though our hearts are in ribbons.

* * *

It is mid-December.

Christmas is coming and the goose is getting fat and the four of us will be together for it, under this wooden roof in New Zealand. For the last time.

Three of us will leave here at the end of the month.

I'm forty-eight and I'm flattened, a cartoon figure against a green screen. Steve and I will play the roles together so we can all see out this final act. We are paper dolls. We are the Rogers of Parnell, Auckland.

I take down the photo of us: my mother and father, Steve, Al, Mae and me, happy faces against a white background. It was the last thing I took down from the walls of our house in Dublin three years ago, and now it is down from another wall, going into bubble wrap again. Another December.

If we took a family photo now, who would be in it?

Maybe I won't take this one back. It won't even have arrived in Dublin and it'll already be out of date. It tells an old story.

* * *

It's Christmas Day. With the born-again enthusiasm of people who know that the end is in sight, Steve and I say all the right words and give all the right looks. We smile and we laugh, wearing party hats. We feel only the right things. Suddenly we can love again. We can love for Ireland. We can love for Christmas.

It's not long.

The four of us talk and eat and drink and sit in the garden and talk and then not talk for a while and then laugh, like a family does.

We walk to the harbour – Steve a little ahead, Al looking around behind, Mae and I pottering in between. Just like before. Smiles and festive greetings are directed at Mae, and then at the rest of us. Still my family. As completely distant and as utterly close as family can be.

In the evening, the nostalgia for us four being together – just us four, simply and only – almost chokes the air, colluding with the Christmas tree in the corner and the festive goodwill and the warmth of the sunlight.

'I wish us both a happy new year,' I say to Steve, as the night closes in. And I mean it.

For the last couple of days, he and I have had very careful short conversations – safe and kind, never steering towards anything too real or dangerous. Too many words could give rise to too many feelings and you might find yourself revealed, uncertain, all your resolve and good sense lost among the wrapping paper and the sweet, burned smells of warm orange and clove.

We are packing it in. Packing to leave each other, to leave this country, this hemisphere, our son, our marriage. Anything that can be left is being left.

Outside the window, the blossoms from our pohutukawa tree are blood-red even in this dark.

* * *

'When you laugh – when I make you laugh – it's like nothing else. It gives me such a lift, even now. Like a child being given a golden star.'

Steve's words dangle in the air, like the Christmas lights. And I love them, like a familiar trinket, but I know we need to take them down and box them away.

This house – this display case – is a different place now that everything's out, everything's on show.

'Now that I'm packing up our lives, it's not the time for you to think that maybe we could work it all out.' I smile at him.

He can entertain the idea. Fanciful and beautiful. Because the die is cast. The tickets are booked.

He puts his arms around me and hugs me close, the rubble of us scattered all around. And I think it's a shame that we couldn't be enough for each other. How I can't make peace with the risk of him, how I'm exhausted by us.

I've realised that life is possible for me without being his wife. That maybe I could accept everything and take him on again, but I can't bring myself to want to, to keep running his show, fearing for what might be. I have made a safe place in my heart for my children and me. I will bed down with them and it will be certain and it will be real.

'I'll be able to see Olivia every second weekend,' he says, his arms still around me.

'That's good. I'm glad.' And I kind of was.

I feel him nod, appreciating me saying it.

And then he lets me go. He stands back and looks about the room, so that the conversation will end there.

Quit while we're not too far behind.

Before it ends in tears.

* * *

I've told myself that my hurt has always been on my daughter's behalf. I don't like to think that it might have been my own envy overtaking me.

Maybe I won't always feel as I do about Jane. I wonder now if she and I might have liked each other, had we met in different circumstances. Maybe a day will come when she drives me only a little way up the wall. Maybe I'll even allow myself to see that she was the one left holding the baby.

* * *

And then Al is gone. From this house for good. Or for bad. For ever.

'It's all downhill from here,' he'd said, half smiling and motioning at the hill that runs from the front of the house to the water. His eyes were damp when he turned away. Just as they were the day Steve and I pulled out of the driveway in Dublin to take Mae for her heart surgery. Leaving him in the garden. He didn't say it then either – *goodbye.* I remember how he pressed his palm against her window at the back of our car. How she met it from the inside with her tiny one. Their hands flat against the glass. Two starfish. A slow high-five.

And now they will be so far from each other, this brother and sister. My children. I have allowed them to be separated. And I want to shout. Shout loud enough to knock the glass from the windows and walls in this kitchen. Stay. Stay with us. I want him to stay with me, me to stay with him. With Mae. The three of us here in the sun. Not just Mae and me back in the damp. Chased into an exposed corner of the Atlantic.

But Steve, Steve needs Mae. And, now that he knows her, he needs Olivia. And they need him.

So Al is the only one who can stay, the only one who is free to do so.

That night I open the door to his bedroom. I look in at nothing, into silence.

I see a photo propped up on his empty desk. It's the one of him on our couch in Dublin, Mae looking up into his face. He is smiling down into hers. Her little arms are around his neck. My children, younger, caught up entirely in each other. He has stuck a pink Post-it to it. His letters are primary-school clear for his sister to read them by herself. 'Love you always, Mae, you big hero. Al xxx'

The pain bends me double.

* * *

I get out my passport. And both of Mae's – Irish and New Zealand. She belongs in both places. And I belong where she is.

Ireland is thirteen hours behind us. With each hour that my parents sleep and I busy myself, I feel how far apart we are.

Going back in time, back to where it's yesterday.

'You'll be halfway home before you've even left,' my father had joked.

Home.

'I've always lived here so I've never really thought of New Zealand as anything other than the place where I just *am*,' Claire had said. I don't remember ever feeling that way about Dublin, about Ireland. So comfortable, so part of it, that it's the place where I just *am*.

But how differently I feel about this place now, about this house, since a tumbling and heavy cloud came to weigh over it, over us. Our cloud. This rented wooden house at the top of a street that sweeps down to the centre of the city, to the harbour. The tips of the triangular sails are still dots of colour visible from its porch – life happening right there, within our reach.

But a new life arrived and a different kind of love happened, and as the cracks spread under us, we stopped making plans for our future here. And this house no longer feels like us at all. We are separate from each other pinned behind its glass, set apart from things here up on the hill. This house is over for us. Our weather has changed.

* * *

'I thought you were already gone! That you'd just left with Mae, without waiting for me.' Steve leans against the bedroom wall, his face pale. 'The rooms were all empty and I was calling and you weren't answering and I couldn't hear Mae or anything, and I just – I thought you'd gone after Al or, I don't know, I panicked and – I don't know what I thought.' Tears fill his eyes. 'Stupid of me. Panicking like that.' He's quiet for a moment, calming down. 'But this is how it will be, Bethy. This is what's ahead now. Me coming into empty rooms, into an empty house, nobody answering, no sounds of anything, just – nothing.'

I stop folding clothes into a suitcase and look at him, feel for him.

'What's happened? What have I done? How can I be fifty and facing into this? I've lost everyone. What a mess. And at fifty.' He marvels at the number, repeating it over and again. 'Everyone knows it. Fifty is not a good age for men, for stress.' He sits on the side of the bed and thinks about himself.

I pack clothes into a suitcase.

* * *

I can't sleep. I think about the doors slammed, the silences after, Mae with her arms wrapped around herself, Al's watchful eyes. All of us losing. I remember the silences in my house as a child – the horrible quiet gaps between words where love is held back, where pain and resentments hide and breed. I think of my mother prattling loudly about nothing, then falling silent when it came to anything real, afraid to ask questions because of what the answers might be.

I get up and look at the suitcases on the floor, at how I might better fit everything in.

Steve wakes with a start.

'Sorry,' I say. 'I can't sleep.'

He stares at me, like I'm someone he may have met before. He's been dreaming. I move across the room and sit next to him. I look into his eyes in the half-light and I can see he's lost – with too many roles to master, he's playing none of them well. And I almost pity him. During this last week, this final crawling week with everything peeled bare, our hands met once in bed. He apologised, and I said nothing. But I have an urge now to reclaim him as my own, for both of us. Here. Just for this last night, in this once-idyllic place, where we once loved each other almost fully.

I put my hand on his chest and he looks at it, feels the charge from it. He reaches up and touches my face, and we kiss.

His hands on me, under me.

Our bodies are attentive, knowing it's the last time. And at three a.m., in the blurred space between an old night and a new day, nobody can be held accountable.

Afterwards we sit outside on the porch steps. My back is to him, my head resting against his shoulder. His arms are clasped around my waist. His legs and mine. Everywhere parts of him around me. Comforting.

A honeymoon pose in the separation stage.

'My father has always adored you, you know,' he says, into the still blackness of the garden.

'I've always adored him too.'

'He told me you were "a real diamond". That it was no wonder I'd had to cross the earth to find you.'

My eyes fill, thinking about Bill as he used to be. Imagining him saying this. I wonder what he'd think of us now if he was capable of it. Perhaps it's for the best that he isn't. I remember him squeezing my hand, telling me I'd survive this. And I will – just not with Steve.

'I'll miss so much – Mae climbing in between us on Saturday mornings, her hair messy and her glasses crooked on her nose, hearing her run across the deck when I'm getting out of my car in the evenings, watching her go down our street on her bicycle, barefoot and speeding away, her chin raised to catch the breeze.'

Our street.

'Not seeing her every day . . .' His voice cracks.

Never seeing Al, I think.

'I'll miss the way you cope, the way you can make sense of things. Of me,' he says now. 'I'll miss our life, you know, the ordinary day-to-day. Our newspaper delivered, the heating on timer, the flowers on the table, all the normal things, like the schoolbags in the hall, the familiar voices when I come in. That's the real stuff, I suppose. You did all of it. *Home*, I guess you'd call it.'

'Family,' I say.

I feel him nod, his head behind mine.

The air is cool and clean but, looking up, I see that the sky is strangely unlit, the stars barely showing themselves – they're glinting and vanishing, on and off, none of them holding out for long, none foolish enough to light us any more.

'You're the planet I orbit around, Bethy. The push-pull of me. What am I going to do?'

* * *

I sit on the stairs and twist my wedding ring round and round. These are my last hours living here. Tomorrow we will leave and we will stop being a couple. And with that, our family as we know it – as our children have known it – will dissolve.

When we arrive back to Dublin, Steve will live on the edge of two families, having it all and having nothing. Fragments in his palms. His father and his son will be together on the opposite side of the world, so he will be blessed among women.

Standing, queuing with our baggage, waiting to be checked in. The two of us. A line of goodbyes in our wake. Mae's hand grips her little Paddington suitcase. Airline stickers and *Please Look After This Bear.*

Steve appears with a trolley. We are travelling together, but everything is separate this time. We have our own suitcases of items and clothing, no longer packed as a collective.

I take my daughter's free hand to ground me.

We will have to piece a version of us back together somehow, us three, but the jigsaw won't be the same. Different edges, a smaller scene.

Everything feels wrong and against nature. We are birds flying north for the winter.

I will come back here with Mae to spend time with Al, not in my home but in his. I wonder if the damage of all of this will be visible in him then. If it will be etched into his face, into his lifestyle.

I'm grateful for the distractions and complications of the airport. Queues, luggage, queues, measured fluids, clear plastic bags, shoes off, shoes on, belt off, belt on, phones and iPads and keys into trays, security checks, queues, restaurant options, cash machines, toilets, lifts, walking, screens changing, walking, queues, numbers.

Following the numbers, walking on out of my marriage.

Panes of glass everywhere as we walk to our gate. Everything reflecting. A burst of rain falls outside, then the sky retreats and is light again. It never settles in the way Irish rain can.

Leaving gives rise to reflection such as this. To comparison, to looking back. I don't want to reflect. Too much is being left, too much is to be faced. There is heavy, settled-in rain ahead. There was promise and beauty in moving three years ago, when I stepped out of my old pale skin and turned from everything I knew. But this time the road ahead looks darker than the one behind. I am leaving the December sun for the winter and I am a child down.

Thankfully there are more gates, more screens. And there are magazines and sweets and drinks to be bought, as though this is the last shop on earth.

Passports, tickets, waiting, walking, sitting and waiting.

For ever passes, then comes the first call for passengers travelling with young children or those requiring special assistance. Mae is almost eight and she doesn't want any help so we stay seated and wait. When our time comes we stand, we queue again and then we shuffle down the pleated tunnel with the other stragglers.

Smiling, welcoming, counting, overhead bins, waiting, toilet doors bending in the middle, three seats – two together, one across the aisle – then sitting. Sitting for the long haul. Mae opens her tray table and sets up her iPad on it.

I'm too tired to think but my mind isn't ready to give up. Thinking is all it wants to do, even though it's of no use. This can't be thought through to some other side where I accept that Olivia and Jane are part of our lives, and where I accept that Al isn't. Where I can trust. There is no through-road to such a place.

'I can drop the ball. Or I can run with it,' Steve had said a few weeks ago, talking about Olivia – his new *development*. I hated the sporting analogy, the way he *faux*-shrugged off his shoulders the life we had built together.

'Oh, Bethy, what have we done?' he asked me this morning. 'All those years together – what have we done?'

Our life had been attacked from the inside. I see now that from the morning when the letter arrived – when I remembered Jane and past deceit – I began to close off, to stay a little separate within the marriage, to hold a part of myself to myself. I turned the safety catch and put a piece of me out of Steve's reach.

Most of the time, it feels like everything between us is utterly broken.

But then there is doubt too. There will always be doubt.

And there have been times this last month – when it has just been us – when it felt we were badly damaged, yes, and barely hanging by age-old threads, but still hanging in, hanging on.

I half listen to an automated voice talk us through life jackets and exits. Cabin crew demonstrate blowing into tiny rubber tubes.

I remember Jane and Steve talking outside, that last day, their faces seeming to me to be so close that they must have been breathing each other's air, sharing each other's words.

And, yet, still there is doubt.

Certainty is Mae and me.

The plane taxis down the runway now, New Zealand shuttling past, speeding up, its landscape blurring. I turn away. I look across the aisle at Steve. He is rolling his shoulders, stretching his neck backwards, forwards. This country goes right to the core of him. And he's leaving it. For his daughter. He closes his eyes. Gone.

'Nobody chooses an affair so they can spend a lifetime on custody matters, financial issues and inadequate parenting,' Claire had said. 'Affairs are for drama and excitement and exhilaration and guilt. That kind of carry-on. To make you feel young and alive and full of anguish and heightened, temporary things.'

The plane rises and rises and breaks through the cloud.

Mae smiles at me. 'You okay, Mama?' Her sensitivity barometer twitching, looking for a read.

'I am, honey. How are your ears? Not popping?'

'No. I'm chewing. See?' She holds a little ball of gum between her front teeth. It's the only time she's allowed to have it so it's precious and worth showing off.

'I always thought that nothing bad could happen once Dad was around,' Al had said, that last day, as he was leaving. 'So it's time I grew up and copped on a bit anyway, Mum. Really.' He'd put his long arms through his rucksack, and shifted its weight into balance on his back. Turned away, then half turned back to me. 'Will you leave your phone on, you know, when you get home – back to Ireland? Like, you know, at night? Just in case I need to talk to you.'

'It'll never be off, Al. Call me anytime.'

His girlfriend Lisa was in her car, waiting at the kerbside.

'And I'll leave mine on too. In case you need me.' He nodded as he spoke.

Maybe it was him that left me in the end. Just as I'd left my parents a few years ago, feeling only relief. The image of my father in the car park as snow fell in November, his arms around Gloria. The silent scene both beautiful and horrifying. My mother in the golf club searching for him, worrying aloud that he would be wondering where she had got to.

I was happy to let it all go – far easier not to despair over his deceit when I didn't have to look at either of them. Maybe Al feels the same.

He is free now. Ready to make himself, to stretch himself, to work off the energy of the city and the friends he has around him, the new ones he will make. Possibility everywhere, he is limitless.

I am his cautionary tale.

The seatbelt sign goes out. Steve is already asleep. The man next to him takes down the tray table and tries to rest on it, lays his head on top of his folded arms.

The plane seems now to be still, as though it isn't moving at all. Suspended in one place, parked in the sky.

I can't feel the pull backwards, the return to the house I grew up in, this flight into the past, to where it is always the day before, always yesterday.

'I have to give up on this,' I had said, that morning on the beach. I was the one to call it, as Steve knew I would.

And who can ever say what's for the best? By the time you find out, it's too late regardless.

I take my folded blanket out of its plastic wrapping. Mae sees and wants hers too. I press the silver circle and my seat makes a barely perceptible recline. I lift her armrest and pat the two flat, gauzy pillows on my lap. She smiles and curls up on me, like a cat, as she has since she was a baby. She sleeps.

So now we are two.

Our life. Doing things a certain way. The particular

patterns and routines of our family broken now. An empty chair. Two empty chairs.

We will create new rituals, our own little family routines. She and I.

The food is wheeled down the aisle, everything sweating in plastic casing. It's nothing I want to eat. And, anyway, it's not a mealtime, not on our clock. Everything is different and feels all wrong. Time itself is wrong.

My marriage is over and this flight can't end fast enough. I am willing the plane on, into the blackness.

And yet. There he is, my husband, the familiar lie of his arm within touching distance for only another few hours. I could touch him, I could smile. But then where would we be?

Feeling my gaze, he turns and looks at me. And in that moment, he has more courage than I do. He does it: he puts his hand out to me across the aisle. I take it and he squeezes gently and closes his eyes. I am slain by this, by the familiarity of his old warmth.   And I think how we have been here before – how we have actually held hands this way, making a bridge over the floor, our hearts heavy, in another time. When we lay in two narrow single beds high up in a hospital building, our three-year-old daughter downstairs in Intensive Care, being kept alive, being kept asleep, being kept apart from this world while thick drains, like clear garden hoses, emptied fluid from her insides. I remember her tiny wrists tied to the railings of the bed to stop her pulling at them out of fear or pain; I remember the lines and the tubes and the mark of a knife wound splitting her in half where her ribs had been sawn open. So that her heart, her broken little heart, could be fixed.

Steve and I lay in the spartan parents' accommodation, holding on to hope and to each other across the brown carpet between our beds, holding hands just like this, making a bridge, while the dark eyes of Padre Pio stared down from the wall, framed above us.

I remember all of this now, here, on a plane over the Pacific Ocean and I squeeze his hand back.

Mae stirs in her sleep, makes a sound, settles again.

'Excuse me.' The steward wants to pass. 'You need to keep the aisle free, please.'

The inside of the plane has become dark. Here and there, overhead reading lights throw small beams. I fall asleep for a while.

I wake up thinking about James, a boyfriend I had before I met Steve, when I still lived with my parents. We were together for two years. The last time we were in touch, I'd been away for a fortnight and I'd phoned his house as soon as I got home. His sister, Amy, had answered. I remember my crazed sense of longing, a need to see him, to squeeze him tightly.

'Hi, Amy. Is James there? It's me.'

'Hi there. Yep. Sure.'

She yelled into the background, 'James. It's Suzie. On the phone.'

The sound of heavy footsteps and then the black receiver being lifted from where it lay upturned on the wobbly wooden table in the hall, and then—

'Hi, you. I was actually just thinking about last night. Mmm.'

So I left him. But, really, he'd already left me. For some Suzie.

And here I am again. My life exploded by some Suzie.

We land and the heat of Dubai is a wall, and I'm glad we're only passing through. Dragging ourselves, weary and out of sorts. Our hand luggage is now a mess of wrappers, the rubble of snacks, and dog-eared magazines.

* * *

It's eight p.m. when we land in Dublin, which makes it nine a.m. tomorrow in Auckland. Al has the jump on us already.

I wonder if an old version of myself is buried somewhere within me, a version that half fits being back here.

She never forgot her roots. Isn't that what they say? To keep you down. To keep you from soaring.

Back to reality now. As if the only reality is the one you're born into.

Can I pull it to the surface? The old me. Like a coat

from the back of a wardrobe. Can I put it back on and will its old skin fit?

* * *

My mother has never missed an opportunity to meet someone coming in on a plane, boat or train. She likes to be the first at the scene. She arrives early to get the best vantage point. She needs to have all the angles. Her eyes dart around, taking in every unsteady pile of suitcases snaking through the sliding doors.

But she is not here.

My father has his back to the doors, is checking the arrivals screen, when we come through. It's been some time, but I know the outline of him immediately, the shape of him, the hang of his left leg – the side of his bad hip – the swing of his long winter coat, and his polished shoes.

My mother would be livid if she knew we had appeared while his back was turned.

* * *

'Sorry to hear about all of this, Steven,' my father says, once we get outside. 'It's a real shame. The whole thing.'

They shake hands.

The icy steel of the air freezes my insides with every new breath.

'I'm sorry too,' Steve says, his eyes filling. 'I really am.'

'No point dwelling on it now. We're all of us human. Beth tells me you're going your own way this evening.'

Mae is huddled into me. Tiredness and the suddenness of the cold are keeping her silent and unaware.

'Yes, I think that's best. I'll take a taxi to a hotel. Let you all have your space. Give my regards to Johanna and –' he breathes deeply, readies himself to speak again '– look after my girls.'

They nod at each other, these two men. These two fathers.

* * *

In the car, my father tells me that my mother looked better before she looked worse. 'She lost a few pounds and was quite delighted with herself. She actually looked very well for a while. Well, for a short while.' His voice cracks so he leaves it at that. He turns on the radio but doesn't drum along using his two index fingers on the steering wheel, like he usually does.

But it's been years. What do I know about what he usually does?

Christmas songs and lights string through villages on the drive home. The rooftops and the lintels between are glossy with rain. Here, where it's still yesterday, where night is beginning to fall. I check my phone – it's December 30th. Traffic lights bleed red into the sky, while the street lamps glow like amber moons.

And then we're coming down my parents' gravel driveway in the dark and it's suddenly all nostalgia and childhood and Santa and warmth, the magic of the cold and the hoping for snow. Silver lights are wrapped around the big hulking tree in the garden and along the front of the house. A dormant part of me awakens.

Mae stirs in the back seat. 'Wow!' she says, her eyes wide now. She hasn't seen Christmas lights against a wintry black sky for a long time. Probably ever, that she can remember.

As I get out of the car, I wonder how I never really smelt the cold before – that clean icy rush – when I lived here, as a child or as an adult. Perhaps it was too familiar to notice, it just *was*.

Mae blows out, raises her hand to the white clouds of her breath. She looks at me and laughs. Everything a marvel.

And then a shock of rain unleashes itself and we run. Run across the shining gravel and up the steps to the front door, smiling at each other, at the cold, at the change in our weather from summer to this baubled darkness. A waxy green wreath, with red holly berries wound through it, hangs from the door's brass knocker. The brass itself is glinting, recently polished.

This front door. So much more than just a front door.

Mae and I stand waiting for my father to unlock it, her dark hair decorated with glistening water beads.

The first of the suitcases scrapes along the floor as I push it into the house. Steve would have carried the lot upstairs. Before. I wouldn't have had to think about their weight. My father drags the others in, shunts them further down the hall. 'That's the last one,' he says, as it slides against the legs of the chair by the piano. The sound echoes off the old high walls and ceiling. My baggage is managing to take up a lot of floor space, despite my having nothing much to show for those years away. Some clothes, a few personal bits and Mae's favourite toys.

And I'm two men down.

I'm distracted by the heat. The temperature is tropical in here, despite the deep frost outside. Every radiator must be on, pumping. I take Mae's scarf and jacket off her, then remove my own. I step into the sitting room. A long garland with red bows at each end is draped across the fireplace. I glance at my watch to check the clock in the centre of it is still fast. It is. By eight minutes. My mother keeping ahead of the game.

I turn and my legs weaken beneath me as I make her out, lying behind me, the entire mass of her so small. She is across the couch, and the parts of her that I can see above the blankets are thin, angular.

'She's only lost the real weight in the last ten days or so,' my father says quietly, from over my shoulder. This is meant to reassure me, but does the opposite.

I could lift her. I could lift all of her right now. I could bundle her to me, this little pile of sticks, and hold her. My mother.

And I'm immediately glad that I'm back here. In this room that I haven't missed once. Back among all of this heavy furniture, among the too many ornaments and gilt-edged frames, among candlesticks and cushions and rugs, and not enough space to be let feel, watched by the photo of my parents taken and hung a lifetime ago, when they were young and without children and smiling at each other, never guessing at the mountains ahead. Everything in the room looks exactly the same. Except my mother.

'Hello, hello!' she says. 'Mae, Beth.' She brings her wizened hands together and smiles. 'I hear you're both going to stay with us for a while.' Her voice is so familiar: it's hers but a kind of bleached-out version. 'I mean, of course you're welcome. Oh, more than welcome! I can't even say how much. It's wonderful to have you here.'

Her words, which had often sliced at me with their barbed, spiky edges, are gentle. So much a part of my life before, my mother's biting remarks at every turn. Her reprimanding tone telling me how to iron in a crease, how to baste a turkey, how to dead-head a geranium, how to defrost my freezer, how to stay married, how to be thinner, how I should be less demanding; her with all of life's answers. And I miss it already. The certainty and black humour of her words, her backbone. Hearing her speak now – little more than a whisper, she who would always be heard even through a slammed door – immediately closes any distance I feel between us.

'You must be tired, Beth. Tired of everything, I imagine.' She puts her hand on mine. 'What a trip to have to undertake. With all that's going on.'

I feel impossibly sad and child-like.

It's just her. No criticism. No false fervour. Just my mother. Laid bare.

'Stay as long as, well, as long as you want.' Her eyes fill, which is not something that has happened often in our lifetime together. We both know. Mae and I will be here for ever. Her for ever.

I still haven't spoken. I don't know where to start, with everything there is to say now.

'It's made my day, my – everything. I just wish it were in better . . . you know. Anyway. Enough of all that.' One arm rises a little, to bat something away. 'You'll have some tea.' She takes my daughter's hand. 'And I have chocolate milk for you, darling Ismae, you beautiful bird. I don't know how you survived that trip! Aren't you the lovely brave girl? And so big now!' She pats Mae's hair, pats the water drops down, then brings her damp and gnarled hand to touch her granddaughter's face. 'Such freshness. I haven't been outdoors for days now. Too cold for me out there. Too cold for me everywhere.'

I put my arms around her, my mother, and hold all of her to me.

And she holds me to her.

* * *

I'm not back an hour and I'm already crying in my parents' kitchen. Warm, fat tears for my mum and Al and Steve and my father, and even for fucking Gloria and Jane, and how the wheels eventually come off everything.

Watching me, my father looks a bit relieved. His face is weary, but he knows how to play a hero. He makes several pragmatic health-related statements, a cup of strong coffee, then moves on to practical talk of us ploughing on, getting through. One foot in front of the other. And I find that I'm nodding along, that I'm up for it. In that moment, I believe I'm the survivor he claims I am.

* * *

The following morning I waken early, despite so little sleep behind me. It's difficult to rest in a new place. A new old place. Especially when you don't know how many nights, how many mornings your mother might have left in her. I'm lying in the single bed of my childhood, which seems cot-like now, a doll's bed. My neck is strained at an angle from the same two-pillow combination always used throughout the house – one hard and flat, the other soft and full, sitting atop each other. I forgot to throw the full one onto the floor as I used to.

The side-table and the lamp with the boned shade, its switch too far down the cord to reach without getting out of the bed. Everything is as it was. My room preserved as though under a plastic film. To keep it fresh, stored. But for what? Not to be used, not to encourage visitors.

I listen to the rain hitting the skylight above me. And, at forty-eight, I feel seventeen again. In every bad way. I am back not-sleeping in this room, a child of my own grown and far away.

All is quiet, so I assume my daughter is not awake yet. She is in the next room – the guest room we called it, although no guests were ever invited.

It would have been my brother's room, had he lived. My brother who never made it to this world alive – who was stillborn when I was eight years old. I picture my mother in her lemon summer dress lying on the floor, like a pregnant rag doll, not long before it happened. Before my brother was born. He would have been forty this year, but the memory of my mother slumped on the floor is as searing as ever.

The always-empty guest room.

Until now. For the next while, it will be Mae's room. She will stay here with me, a new half-sister a few hours away, her full-brother a world away, and her father alone – or something like it – carving up his time between her and another daughter.

* * *

I sit in the kitchen in what was always considered to be my seat. The others are tucked in under the table at perfect distances from each other. It's still dark outside. I've seen no brightness since I landed here. The window reflects back the hanging light fitting and what's here inside. Two of everything.

All is clean, pristine. As ever. But now there's a

chemical smell to it, a new dimension of clean. Hospital-level hygiene.

No germs, please. We're waiting for death.

A magnet I haven't seen before is stuck to the fridge: a small plastic square with *Prayer for the Sick* in an italicised font, and a floral border around a verse. It makes me uneasy.

How long has she been at this stage? The being-prayed-for stage. That someone would see this magnet and think of her. And actually buy it.

The Beefeater magnet I bought in London in 1986 is gone. A souvenir from a time I never want to think about. From a day in Ealing over thirty years ago that she and I had told ourselves was for the best. I don't think it had lost its stick. She must have thrown it out. Maybe in an effort to come over to my side, to help me forget.

I get up to fill the kettle. The water explodes from the tap in short, repetitive bursts, as it always has. The only vigour left in the place.

* * *

My father hadn't realised she was so ill. 'I mean, with hindsight,' he says, 'there had been some signs but I hadn't seen them. I didn't let myself, I suppose.'

My mother suspected it was bad before the results came back but she hadn't said. 'I've always hated hospitals and being around the sick, you know that. I'd rather be here, at home, away from the broken bodies and the false hope.'

She pauses a moment, catches her breath. 'I've been lucky in my life. And with you and Ismae and your father here now, I'll be more . . . ready.' She smiles sadly and her waxy skin tightens, revealing her teeth. Her face is smaller so they look huge, wolfish.

She puts her hand around mine and gives a squeeze. I barely feel it.

* * *

'Hi,' Steve's voice answers. So familiar, so reassuring to hear it.

'Hi. Can you talk?' *Are you alone?*

'Yes, what's up?' The volume from a radio or a TV is turned down. Knowing the patterns of his lifetime, I decide it's a TV. 'You okay?'

'Not really.' I shake my head, even though we're on the phone. 'My mum has cancer.'

And then he is here. In the kitchen where I grew up. Solid and steady. And he knows me. He knows my mother. He knows what to say and when to say nothing. He remembers how she takes her tea. That my father prefers coffee. He has both the strength and the sensitivity to manoeuvre her on the couch so she is more comfortable. Which makes me feel more comfortable.

'How bad?' he asks me, in the hallway.

'Really bad,' I say. 'How did I not know? How did I not pick up on it?' I'm quiet for a moment. 'Too caught up in other things,' I answer myself. I remember now that it was my father who Skyped the last time, and I realise it's been weeks since I saw my mother's face on my screen.

'I'll take Mae out for a while, give you guys some time. Whatever you need, just let me know.'

He is still my husband, because he was once my husband. And these things are a lot simpler to get into than out of.

Trust is fragile and breaks down, but still love is stubborn.

And then his phone rings. He looks at the screen and puts it on silent. Back into his pocket. 'Take all the time you need, Beth.' He hugs me close and is gone, hand in hand with our daughter.

* * *

It's hours later before I realise that the window blinds in the sitting room stay lowered all of the time. That it's not just in the evenings and early mornings. My mother is dying. So of course this is what's done. Blinds like closed eyes. My mother and my marriage, failing together. Mirroring each other's demise.

* * *

The year is ending. 2017. I think about the last weeks and months. So much change, barely a single thing left as it was. And it seems fitting, in the bleakest of ways, it seems horribly *right* to me that this period would end with a considerable event. With a huge full stop.

The death of a mother. What's more final than that? It's the thick, heavy line drawn under all things, under flux. An end to the very life that made you.

* * *

She's kinder now. Or maybe it's that she's somehow happier. More still. No longer manic with trying to seize and maintain some form of control. Calm.

She is the queen of her illness, the centre of the room.

But it might just be the medication.

'Marriage is an impossible business, darling. The other person – your beloved – will always let you down. Disappoint you. Whether they mean to or not.'

Although her voice is a quiet rasp, I think she's about as certain as I've ever heard her. I look down at the heavy rug on the floor, its swirling pattern so familiar. So much swept under it. Despite her sad diligence down through the years, some hints and suspicions had always managed to seep out from beneath its woven corners.

'All this time, since I first met your father really . . . I realise now that I've thought his thoughts and held his opinions, as if they were my own. But lately, during these last weeks, I've had lots of thoughts – different ones, thoughts of my own – and, as painful as some of them have been, there's definitely a freedom in it. It's taken seventy-seven years and this beastly illness for me to learn to think for myself.' She stops, closes her eyes, makes an effort to breathe more deeply, to regulate the pattern. Her eyes open, and she is ready to speak again. Dying to speak. 'I love your father, I always have. But there are other things to think of now. And other ways of seeing the world. And do you know? Sometimes he's wrong. Quite wrong. And he needs to be told. And that goes for Steve too. He has been wrong. And you, Beth, must do what you feel to be right.'

Her bones, like her voice, are weakened now, yet with these words, she takes some of my weight. I didn't need her permission to leave my marriage, but it comes as a relief to know I have it.

And then she says, 'But if I were you, I wouldn't let him go.'

* * *

Her friends visit. They sit in chairs near the couch, where my father and I have arranged her, according to her specifications. The result is her reclining, starlet-style, in a silken robe in front of the open fire. But looking thin and wretched, with blankets piled up to her waist.

She pats her hair now and again, fixing what's left. Old habits. The habits of the old.

She's pale. But it's not only the pallor of illness, it's because her skin colour has faded. Her tan is gone. She isn't olive-skinned, as I'd thought – she was just tanned.

All this time. Groomed to a natural brown. She's actually fair, like me. She just hid it.

In a curious sort of offertory procession, the friends bring grapes, cards, gardening magazines. One brings a scented candle. No flowers, though. Bad for the air in the room. No flowers for the living. However, once you die – nothing but flowers. You just have to wait.

My mother slowly brings her nose down to appreciate the candle. 'Lavender. How lovely.' Everything is slow and quiet. She smiles her thanks.

And then she side-nods at me. *Another candle, Beth. Just what I need.*

I place it on the coffee table, thinking I'd give anything now to hear her familiar clipped tone: 'Lavender! How lovely! It's such a shame I'm sensitive to it. But you weren't to know. One can't be expected to remember all their friends' vagaries! I'm sure I'll find someone to give it to. Everybody loves a candle.'

Today the drugs make her nauseous so she doesn't even try any of the biscuits or snacks that my daughter carries in on plates. Mae is the primary diversion and I'm glad she's here. I touch her face and smile at her, and I feel better. Always my worry stone.

I ask them about their children, their grandchildren, their golf and their husbands, so that my father doesn't have to. He can just to and fro, carry a teapot, poke at the fire. My mother listens, nods. I bring up safe topics. I don't mention my own unsafe one – my husband, his other daughter. And my mother's pressing illness and their own good breeding prevents them raising it, here in this furnace of a room.

She tells them how much of a shame it is that she never got to make the trip to New Zealand with my father, the one she had planned so precisely. They make soothing sounds and look pityingly at her, then at me. It's a pity party.

One at a time, each of them rests a hand on her arm and says something to her directly, earnestly, before they file out of the room. At the front door, I tell them I will keep in touch. Let them know.

She doesn't mutter about the crumbs or ask me to vacuum as soon as they leave. She is no longer beating her wings about things she can't control. She has loosened her grip and found her freedom.

Breathe. Release.

But then that cough.

* * *

Laughter. I turn off the kettle to listen. It's my parents. I move out into the hall, nearer the warmth of the sound. My mother and father, laughing. Really laughing. Hers is more of a whisper but I can hear there is still some strength in her, despite everything. They are in the lounge, the door ajar. I realise how unfamiliar the sound of my mother laughing is to me.

For most of their marriage, my father tolerated her. She worked tirelessly to keep him comfortable, well fed and efficiently organised so that he wouldn't stop just-about-tolerating her one day. She took whatever he gave, which was the worst of him mostly, because having any of him meant that at least someone else wasn't. She worked selflessly and with focus on the one project for her entire adult life: preventing Dermot O'Connor leaving her.

Indeed, she managed him so thoroughly that, a number of years into their relationship, it became the case that he could no longer take care of himself. His life skills deserted him. Perhaps his memory of them had gone from selectively hazy to just hazy. Regardless, my mother had succeeded in making herself my father's PA so he couldn't do without her.

In return for her dedicated, unswerving service, Johanna O'Connor was rewarded with decades of painful longing and emotional neglect, which she grew accustomed to. She felt tenuously loved at best. So she tried harder, cleaned more, dressed better, got up earlier. Her chest rose and her back straightened if he praised her at all, as one might a member of staff, such was her need for even the most mundane acknowledgement by her darling.

I wonder how much she knew. About Gloria. About others. How much she knows now, laughing in the next room.

Her eyes were always so tired, her face a collection

of powdery lines and crevices, while my father's stayed almost untouched by age or stress. He was a man with the upper hand.

But lo! Now, here it is, the golden egg of notice and love! She has won his heart at last, uncovered a devotion that has lain dusty for decades.

Life has forced her to focus on something else, backed her into a space where she has to concentrate on herself. And this has made my father jealous. Her energy, her focus is no longer his alone. Now he wears the face of a man who feels his love under threat, looking significantly older – he for whom time had previously stood still. Grieving already, knowing and waiting. Having to wait, something in itself entirely foreign to him. Learning.

Although there will be little time to observe the new order, the table has turned between them. And my mother, gaunt and slight, is finally seated at its head.

If only she hadn't been so selfless. If she hadn't abandoned herself to him so entirely and for so long, would he have been different? Might he have loved her and her only, if not for the confidence her adoration gave him? The confidence to keep secrets, the confidence to be with someone else.

* * *

'I'm going to pass on soon, my love,' she says to me. 'And I've been thinking about your brother quite a bit lately, can you believe? Perhaps it's not that unusual to wonder about these things when we know our number's about to be called. I've been wondering if I might see him, if he might be waiting for me. Is that foolish, do you think? Oh, but what a delight, Beth – an actual *miracle*, I suppose you'd call it – if any of that Heaven business turns out to be true.' Her voice is throaty and broken, but her words come quickly. Tumbling out while the going is good, while her breaths allow it.

I don't want to scatter her thoughts by interrupting so I just take her hand and listen.

'My tiny baby, waiting to see me! The last time I thought about him so much was after Ismae was born, when I felt the silence around you – that horrid silence of people not knowing what to say – and I remembered it. I remembered it exactly from all those years before. When I came home from the hospital with no baby – the shocking quiet. But now maybe I will see him, maybe I will get to have my son. Do you think? It does seem ridiculous, though, no? When you think of it. Do you think there's anything in all of that? Imagine it!' She smiles a little, closes her eyes for a minute, and then continues: 'And maybe even my friend Sarah Winston and I together again in the evenings, able to hear what they're all really saying down here. What they say about each other when they get home from that bloody club and the knives come out. What a hoot that would be! And, of course, your father. I could keep a close eye on him. For the first time.' A little chuckle. The humour of the finish line.

My mother thinking about the dead. The ones she wants to see, the ones she can live without. Die without.

She will die before my father. He will outlive her. This fact in itself is hard for me to stomach. He's been outliving her since they met.

* * *

Time passed. We let it pass. And now she is frail. Her tiny body needs lifting into the armchair.

I wish Al was here to say goodbye. And yet I don't – he's had enough goodbyes, enough losing people in his life. I don't want him to fly this far into another darkness.

'I'm sorry, Beth.'

'For what, Mum?'

'For not being better. For trying to fold you up into something, into what I thought you should be. For thinking I knew how you should live. What did I know about living?'

'Mum, really, it's—'

'No, please. Let me. I've been waiting to say this to you for the last couple of weeks. I'm sorry for always grating off you. For never believing in what you wanted.'

Her eyes are watery and grey, the blue leached out of them. When did that happen? When did the colour go from my mother's eyes? Would I have left if I'd known this would happen so soon? 'What did I know either, Mum, about how to live? What do I know now? My husband has a child who was born during our marriage. And I'm back where I started, but with less. Less people, less money, less everything. I mean, really, what the fuck do I know about anything? About the human heart.'

She lets my bad language go, doesn't wince or tell me I sound like a fishwife.

'You know, Beth, in the past I'd have told you that life is a struggle and love a test of endurance. That those who are steadfast and committed and forgiving are rewarded. All that righteousness.' She stops. I wait. She starts again, even quieter now. 'But I don't know if I think that any more. I'm at the end of my test. The finish is just ahead, and I've given it a lot of thought. I think you should tell Steve that he must offer every support to the young girl, but as for her mother – this *Jane* – well, really, she needs to just fuck off.'

I gasp and laugh. As though the Pope himself has come into the room in his pointy hat and sworn.

And then she laughs. And wheezes and laughs. And I'm still laughing as I hug her.

Sweet release.

And I know that this is a moment I will remember.

* * *

My mother finding poems on loose sheets hidden within the pages of books my father was reading. Poems he had written. And her thinking, knowing, that they weren't written about her. So many years ago now. I will remember that too.

* * *

I wake up for the fourth time that night to the sound of my mother's rasping breaths. She sleeps for much of the day now.

Sleeping, waking, sleeping, waking. In fits and starts. I feel the rushes of love and the sweeping extravagances of sorrow that watching someone die gives rise to.

The house has lost all rhythm.

* * *

'Do you want me to put on the TV? There are quizzes and things in the afternoon, I think.'

'No, thank you, darling.' Her voice is small. 'The only people who put the television on during the day are those without purpose, drinkers, and the very ill.'

I smile and put the remote down.

'I realise I'm at least one of those things but I don't need to behave like it. I'd rather do a crossword.' She slowly takes a pen between her bony fingers. 'Although I actually only do the word searches now. I don't have the concentration for all the clues and the ruminating.'

She looks down, and after what seems like for ever, she slowly draws a faint and wobbly ring around three letters.

* * *

Barely a week passes, and she is just a husk, hung with flesh. I stay awake with her every night. Keeping her hours. Mae sleeps. Keeping a child's hours.

I don't sit up on my mother's bed any more. I worry that her tiny frame might roll down the hill created by my weight on the mattress, depressing it.

I remember her wanting to call a priest after Mae was born, in case he might be able to perform a miracle. To change reality. To somehow pray away the Down syndrome. And sitting here now, on a chair by her bed, I understand it. The desperation that allows you to entertain the possibility of a miracle against all reason. To say words into the sky in the hope of changing what's staring back at you: to refuse reality.

My mother is dying. I sit beside her and speak at the ceiling, hoping my words will make it into the sky. Make it up to wherever miracles are made.

Maybe she will live.

* * *

She had a quiet death. Peaceful, my father is telling people, and I suppose that's true. Yet it was violent in its own way, her last moments full of a frightening brutality. Her chest stopped rising, and the sound of her laboured breaths, which I could never get used to, suddenly ceased. The silence was fierce and horrifying. I hope she didn't sense my fear. I didn't sense hers.

Hers. My mother's. Johanna's.

She was gone in an instant. She just *stopped.*

Stopped dead.

It was during the night. Death always seems to slide in when it's dark. Even its smell is darkness.

I stood, leaning on the back of the chair, holding it down. Preventing myself from throwing it across the room.

The mass growing inside her got the better of her, took all of her.

The pain inside me was a shattering.

* * *

My mother has been dead for two days. I have been back in Ireland for sixteen, including this one. I was gone for three years. All these numbers adding up to what?

Nothing.

Despite ourselves, despite living in opposition to each other for much of our lives, the bond between my mother and me had endured. Love endures. The clean pain of her loss burns and surprises me.

I sit on the couch where she was lying that first night I arrived back here. In from the airport, without a husband or a son. Mae and I, two little match girls brought in out of the cold. That was just over a fortnight ago. A lifetime ago, as it turns out.

* * *

'Your mother made me her whole world. And she made herself a rock for me, something to always come back to. She knew I needed that certainty.' My father has his back

223

to me and is looking out through the kitchen window, speaking at it. 'Her love was single-minded, you know – she never wavered. She was a force of a woman and her love for me was always golden, even though I didn't deserve it.'

It was true that she'd been the strength in their marriage. The relationship would never have survived if it'd been up to my father to tend it. To do any more than throw it a scrap now and again. She was its backbone, whatever the cost to herself.

'I didn't deserve her at all, you know,' he says, turning towards me.

I don't say anything.

* * *

I'd only ever seen one body, when I was eight and my friend Natalie's mother had died. She didn't look like herself, not like the Mrs Dunne I'd known, lying there rigid among the cream silk lining. Her face wore a look of piety that was unfamiliar to me and she was overly made-up, all orangey cheekbones. She was in some kind of jacket with a fur collar that I'd never seen on her before either. Maybe it wasn't a full jacket – it might have been just a big fur collar. Nobody was going to pull back the shiny sheet to check. Her hands were high on her chest, bound together by a string of pearlescent rosary beads that gleamed, their links clean silver. Probably bought for the solemn occasion. To the side of her face was a drawing of their family that Natalie had done. Her mother looked more like herself in the drawing than she did that day in the coffin.

My mother looks like herself, though, in that she is gaunt and weak and grey. Exactly as she has been this last week. Her true and worst self, ravaged and small. It's harder now, staring in at death, to believe in any part of her living on, or to conceive of a soul or a spirit or a trace of energy vacating this shell in time to ignite a spark elsewhere. Meeting her infant son, seeing an old friend, watching my father – it's ridiculous even to wish for. But I do.

* * *

Flowers everywhere now. Free to breathe. Let in, having waited weeks. Some are bouquets in cellophane tied with white ribbon, some are circular wreaths with expectations of being placed near the centre of the action.

They add to the thickness of the air, which is already heavy with death and the smell of cold meats and rows of sandwiches under plastic. No eating yet. That comes later, with the chatting, when my mother is gone. Awkward to eat and chat while a corpse wearing make-up lies in a box beside you.

Steve stands with his arm around me and I feel supported and known. My mother would have been glad, especially in front of this suburban golf crowd. He holds my hand at the house, in the car, walking into the church. As though we are in love. And for a short while I forget and think we are.

A lot of coughing and nose-blowing. The throat-clearing and the rustling movements take a few minutes to peter out. I am conscious of sitting upright, my legs crossed, like my mother would. But by the end of the service, I am slouched and sniffling, huddled against Steve.

A long line of people queue to kiss my father and me. To smile at Mae. To shake hands with Steve. To enquire after Al. I stand but feel bare, too much of me absent to represent myself in any certain way. I don't know what I say. I feel my husband's – Steve's – arm strong across my back.

There are more people in the house than I've ever seen here before. My parents' house. My father's house now, I suppose. Men stand around the walls speaking in low voices. Women touch each other's arms and are grave. Someone is trying to find more cups. A voice wonders where best to put down the last tray of cold meats. So much life but so little energy, everything drained and colourless.

Steve stands next to me, keeping me together.

The kettle whistles on in the kitchen, keeping the side up.

The eating starts. Louder chatting follows.

The kettle keeps busy. Someone makes more tea and coffee.

I smile, thinking of my mother's habit of humming and hawing over cappuccinos and skinny lattes, wondering at green teas and turmeric, asking questions about the source of the coffee beans, eventually handing back the menu, deciding against having anything at all. Settling into her seat, a martyr with her arms crossed over her chest.

I'll go without. You enjoy yours.

But just as the waitress is escaping from view, deciding to call her back.

'Excuse me!' across the floor. 'Heavens, she's light on her feet! Excuse me! Yes. Yes, you. Can you please – I've actually changed my mind.'

Smiling about her now, waiting to order.

'There you are. Now, I've actually decided that I'll just have a cup of hot water. Please. That'll do.'

And calling after her again: 'You don't need to bother with a slice of lemon in it or anything nice like that, if it's going to put you to any trouble.'

My mother. Sent to try us.

'It's Jane,' Steve says suddenly, beside me.

I swing around, instantly back in the room, expecting to see her in an elegant black trouser suit.

'No. Here. On the phone,' he says, and shows me the screen. I see her name blinking, *Jane Marshall,* and realise I've never seen it written before. Her first and second names together.

I'm grieving. My mother has just died. My mother. And yet I still care about this woman. I still have space to think of her. Here, on this day.

What is wrong with me?

He switches his phone off and puts his arm around my shoulders. In my desperation, every instinct I have tells me to cling to him, that I have my footing when he's around. He holds me close and here, in this house of my childhood, I feel myself being guided back to him.

'Johanna liked films so we decided recently, when she first became unwell, that we would have a nice evening at the cinema.' Everyone has assembled in the lounge and my father is standing in front of the fireplace, speaking. 'She chose what she wanted to see and we went along for the first time in many, many years. Oh, it's all changed, these days, with the bigger seats, and the sound is so clear, and there's even a bar now so she could have a glass of wine when we sat down. Anyway, she was charmed by it all. And then the programme started, and unfortunately there was someone muttering behind us from the very start. On and off, this muttering continued for the whole film. I was quite irritated and couldn't stop myself turning around and glaring. I became completely hung up on the rudeness of the person behind me because I wanted the evening to be special for her.' He smiles, looks down for a moment, gathers himself.

'But Johanna, she didn't mind that much. She was so happy to be out. Happy to be in the big seats, her hand on mine, just the two of us. And she thanked me, she thanked me for taking her to see a film. Down the road to the cinema. That was all she wanted. And I, honestly, I could have wept then and there for not having taken her more.' His voice cracks and he rubs his eyes under his glasses. 'For not being there more. With or without the muttering.' He is crying now. My father is crying. I am as surprised by his tears as I am moved by them. They stream in lines from his eyes and one drops to the floor from his jawbone. I look away, wondering at my own discomfort.

A smattering of applause and some words of encouragement come from the men standing around the walls. One raises his glass. 'To Johanna. May she—'

'No, not yet. That's not the end,' my father says, and rubs at his cheeks brusquely, cutting off the toast-maker. 'That's not all. You see, when we got up to leave the cinema, I put my coat back on and heard the muttering again. Nearer now, right beside me. But everyone was already filing down the stairs. It was coming from my coat pocket. From my phone. I had left the radio app on the whole way through the film.'

Oh, the assembled enjoyed that. And those gathered around the walls had to have another drink after hearing it.

'My Johanna,' he's smiling now, 'she just laughed and laughed. As much as I'd ever heard her laugh before.'

He is the one to raise his glass: 'To my wife and her wonderful laugh.'

'Your wife and her wonderful laugh.'

And I really hope she can see us all, see herself being celebrated in this way.

Mae is asleep, and the house is dark and quiet. Steve and

I are in the kitchen. I'm sitting in my usual spot while he's tidying and fixing and, from the back, he looks kind and capable. He turns and hands me a mug of tea.

'And here.' He pushes a bowl of olives towards me. 'At least eat these, please. You've had next to nothing all day, Bethy.' He brushes my hair from my forehead.

I start into the olives, spitting the pits into my hand, working my way through the entire bowl, while he sweeps and mops and scrapes and cleans and covers and refrigerates and saves me.

Did my mother do this? Did she give us this opportunity to be close, this chance for him to be kind? To remind me?

He is beside me now and I let my head lean against his chest. He loops his arm around my waist. I remember her telling me how she wouldn't let him go. I allow myself a moment's fantasy about her new life up in the clouds somewhere, and I smile, wondering how she's coping with not being able to instruct him to get into the corners with the mop. I open my mouth to tell him this, but he speaks first.

'It's my weekend in London. This one. And I've been really looking forward to seeing her. Olivia. I'm sorry – I know you're not in the mood to hear this right now.'

My stomach lurches.

A spectre at the window.

'It's okay,' I say. 'Of course you have been. But it's Saturday now, isn't it?' I'm not sure: the days have been jumbling onto each other, climbing on top of me.

You can't go. Don't go. It's too late now. Is it too late?

'Yes, but I wouldn't have dreamed of not being here for you and Mae today. And for your dad.'

'It's meant everything, Steve. I don't know how I'd have got through it without you. Really. Thanks.'

'Don't mention it. Please. And Jane understood. She sends her condolences.'

I nod.

'I'm going to take the early flight tomorrow morning, so all's not—'

'Oh.'

'I'll finish up here and get going. Is that okay?' We stand close and he puts his hands to my face. 'You think you'll be all right, honey?' He looks into my eyes, this man I married twenty years ago, and I hold my breath. 'I'll call in when I get back on Monday evening.'

And then he kisses my cheek, close to my mouth, and I feel my eyes close, and my already broken heart surprises me by breaking again.

I go upstairs to the guest room, kick off my shoes, and get into the small bed beside my daughter. I wrap myself around her, a big crescent circling a little one.

I waken a few hours later, wearing my mourning dress, my daughter in my arms. She is my ballast.

* * *

I take a picnic blanket from my dead mother's cupboard, half expecting the old her to appear behind me and tut-tut about ruining the pile, about needing to refold the others now I have upset them. A cardboard box to the side is a recent addition, in that it's been put there since I moved away. Lifting a flap I see it's full of photos, old ones, the kind with creases cracking through them, breaking up young and familiar faces. The kind of photos I imagine I'm supposed to cherish now. I close the box again and then the cupboard. I'm not ready for all that – to immerse myself in her life, to prod at the bruises of my grief.

The blanket around my shoulders, I sit on the front step looking out at the gravel driveway. My father has disconnected the Christmas lights so now the black is immediate and complete. But the sky is clear so I see the stars above me, cut like ice chips. More stars than I can ever remember here before.

I can't make out my mother's flowerbeds in this dark, but I know they're there, over by her parked car, and preserved in the frost. Her snowdrops have managed to push their delicate, shy heads through the snap of the cold every January since my childhood. But perhaps this year they won't, shrivelling to nothing on my watch.

* * *

So this is the worst time. Everybody says it. Between the demise of my marriage and my mother, and my son being as good as gone from me, this is the worst time. They say.

It will get better, though. They say that too.

Not because my marriage will right itself or my mother will appear to me in a vision or my son will move nearer, but because of Time. Time, and it being a healer.

I want to say that Time is also a killer, but I suppose that's to be expected of me at the moment because, of course, this is the worst time.

* * *

'Everything will be all right,' my father says, giving my leg a quick pat.

'I'll mind you,' Mae says to him, her head tilted to the side, her face serious.

My daughter isn't saddened by my mother's death – old people are meant to go to Heaven. Especially sick ones. They are meant to die, so they can be happy again.

My father smiles. 'You will save my life,' he says to her.

And I feel pityingly, overwhelmingly sad, sitting here on the couch, the three of us in a row. Without Mae and me, it would just be my father here, alone with his thoughts, with the choices of his past.

'I am a doctor,' she says. 'Let me give you a check-up.'

'Oh, I see. Well, certainly.' My father's voice is tender.

'First, I'll listen to your heart,' she says, putting her ear to his chest. 'It sounds a bit slow.'

She sees me watching, vacant. Looking at nothing, really. I'm miles away. 'I love you, Mama.' She brings me back.

'I love you, Mae.'

'All day long.'

'All day long.'

She will save me too, my hands held up to her steady flame.

* * *

Moving through the kitchen, turning off lights. How strange to be the last one to bed every night. No Al, no Steve, no distant television or kettle sounds. No screen door closing. No screen door. Just the wind outside stirring things up.

* * *

It's easier to imagine Steve and me apart when I don't see him. When I don't look into his dark eyes, don't see the shape and mass of him, don't see his ease with Mae – her love for him written all over her face.

When we're together, it seems ridiculous that we aren't still Steve and Beth, the pairing so familiar.

Parting and coming back. Parting and coming back. Like waves breaking.

Some days I just want his arms around me. To forget what's been.

And other days I just want him to walk away, walk off the earth. So long.

'I miss you all of the time. As my wife, but also as my

friend,' he says, the last few words maintaining a distance. 'My corner feels very empty without you, Beth.'

That's when I notice that, most of the time, my corner feels just the same as before.

* * *

I'm parked in Vesey Hill, staring at our house. The house we still own. It looks the same as the others, which is to say bored and hopeless, with a vast and tidy front. They are all tended in their rows, stiff with competition. Ours looks as broad as I remember it, although the proportions now seem wrong. The windows are small, the spaces between them much too big, and the front door is narrow. A wide, unfriendly face with mean features, eyes too small to see anything, really.

And yet I can appreciate that it's also perfect in a way, certainly more than before: these tenants are its rightful dwellers. Two tall lollipop topiaries frame the door, which has been painted a high-gloss black. So much more than a front door. I imagine what's behind it now is a particular kind of perfect too.

I am here to check in on our property, to put the low-level frighteners on the renters and all that, but I can tell there's no need. The house is full of itself, such is their attention to it.

I get out of the car and stand, taking everything in. The road turns sharply and disappears towards the boundary, towards the commanding gates of the estate, which keep us all held inside, safe. Which keep the delicious messiness and blather of life out.

The three of us lived here for years, Steve, Al and I. And for five more after Mae was born. The living by numbers, the set patterns of this community – everywhere inaction, yet our neighbours so busy and enthusiastic about maintaining it. *It*. What? A tidy nothingness. A malaise eventually crept into our house, circled through it and sat, like fog.

In the end, to live an honest life while also staying so fully inside the lines was impossible for me.

A feeling of pointlessness that I haven't had since I left Vesey Hill sweeps over me now, standing here. And I remember that Steve couldn't bear this place either. He said it drove him to madness.

Well, it drove him somewhere.

For a second, I think about burning it down, watching our house burn to the ground, clean. I fantasise about the scale of the flames – about the neighbours standing out on the street, transfixed. Our every window and shutter ablaze, the house spitting charcoal up and out, into the sky above, sending up a flare that would be visible beyond the gates, visible even down the hill in the rest of the town. Visible in places where my neighbours rarely go, where properties are smaller and prices lower.

I imagine I hear them:

Well, there now, you see? The only house that's rented out in Vesey Hill, and it's on fire.

You see? It's just not right. Who would dare not to live in this home, in this desirable enclave, among us?

This is what happens when you don't value things. Everything gets destroyed in the fire. All is lost.

I'd never want to live here again, among the women with anxious, made-up faces and the men trying to keep their hair. The white-knuckle cult of it all. I'd take messiness and blather over it any day.

'Beth! Beth! Hello there!' Anna has seen me first so I can't turn or hide. She kisses the air at both sides of my face. Here on the street in Vesey Hill where, of course, nothing is on fire. And never will be.

Anna, who values appearances in people, and improvements in homes above all things, still here, still missing nothing. Still wearing spotless, shouting-white tennis shoes, the deathly vigilant queen of the cul-de-sac.

'Oh, Beth. How *are* you? It's been so long!' Her smile is wide. And I know her delight is real – she loves drama, the darker the better. It makes her tremble.

'What a *shock* you must have got. My goodness! Steve having a child!' She goes straight for the jugular. 'I don't mind telling you there were quite a few whispers doing the rounds at the school gates there for a while. Your ears must have been burning. Moirah, Saoirse and I talked about little else for a fortnight. We couldn't get our heads around it. I still can't bear to imagine it. A child. And a little *girl* at that!' She puts her hand to her face and shakes her head, bearing to imagine it, relishing it, wanting to lie down and make fucking snow angels in the big sorry heap of it.

I remember the last time I saw Anna. The day we were leaving for New Zealand, when she came over to say goodbye. Her voice so loud and certain. Getting louder as she told me about Steve. About him being spotted by her husband that night in London, about how *preoccupied* he was with a *good-looking blonde woman*. And her smile as she said it, standing on my cobble-locked doorstep, minutes before we left for the airport, minutes before we would get out, get off this hill. Not realising that I already knew about Jane, she was wicked enough to have me find out that way, on that last day.

And now here, in front of me again. Her pinched little face and the accordion of tiny lines around her mouth.

'And Steve?' she says, her lips all a-quiver. 'How is *he* doing? Not that you care, I'm sure. I said to the girls that I'd never hope to be right in situations like this, that I'm not one to say I told you so, but I think you'll remember that I did.' She wags a finger close to my face. 'The *very day* you were leaving here to go off to God knows where with him.'

'To New Zealand,' I say. And I won't forget what you did.

The girls. Discussing my husband and his affair, picking through it, embellishing the little they knew and inventing what they didn't. They wouldn't have dwelled on it with their men, though, in case it was contagious, in case the gated-in husbands might like the sound of it, want a slice of this life off script. They might envy Steve Rogers and his younger blonde.

'*I knew*. I just *knew* you were biting off more than you could chew.' Her hand is over her heart now. 'And here you are, back where you started.'

Moirah comes out through her front door on the opposite side of the street. Her precise walk almost breaks into a run to get to us, to get to the news.

Oh, the juiciness of it! The plump, overripe juiciness of the whole tale. And the subplot – the undercurrent of the ever-present disabled daughter! The comparisons, the pity. And they who had been on to it, who'd known about the blonde, who'd heard about Steve being spotted with her, before I did. These women who had opened their glossy doors wider to let the teller in, to let the scandal in, breathing it down while they pressed on the Nespresso. Safe in their giant houses, clinging to their kitchen islands.

We were considered different enough before this. Our family. But now – now the dishonour is tantalising.

'And as if you didn't have enough on your plate already.' Moirah jumps into the conversation, elbows out, making room. She looks well, or well-*maintained*, I suppose, in her dry-clean-only browns and taupes, her make-up heavy in the street's mid-morning light. She kisses the air beside me twice, clasping her hands around mine. Her hand cream leaves a slick of grease that I want to wipe down my jeans.

'And how *is* little Mae? Sure it's probably all beyond her, the poor thing, which is a small mercy. I just can't come to terms with it myself. And then,' her voice quickens, so much to mention, so much to pity, 'your mother dying too. I mean, honestly. What a terrible run you've had. But, then, it was always one thing after another with you, ever since I've known you. And every time you'd spring back up again. You're amazing! One of life's copers. But, of course, that's why these things happen to you. Because you can handle them. I'd be useless!' She laughs at her fortunate uselessness. 'And at least you were here to spend some time with your mother at the end. Which is something wonderful to have come out of it all.'

The inanity of her. Of all of this. Running on and on and going nowhere. How had I lived among it? Listened to it?

'In a way,' Moirah closes her eyes – the point she's about to make is profound, 'one could argue that it's quite a lovely thing for Steve.'

Anna looks at me to see how I might take this.

'Not that what *he* wants is anyone's primary concern.' Moirah's eyes snap open and she gives a joyless little scoff. *What a shit he is! Hilarious!* 'But you know, Beth, it could well be something lovely for him, something positive in your lives. I know it mustn't seem that way now, but perhaps it will. With Time.'

There it is again. Time. The Healer.

'He already has his boy.' She is still talking. 'How is Alex by the way? And now he has another girl, a little girl he can enjoy the usual things with.' She strides on. 'And I'm *suuuuuure*' – she lengthens the word: she is indeed rather certain – 'that one day, *you*'ll enjoy doing normal girlie things with her too. And that'll be lovely.'

Lovely. Everything's lovely.

Anna's eyes are darting between us, a dark glee causing her to shiver. 'I agree,' she says. 'You should try to see this – see *her*, sorry I don't know her name?'

Nice try. I say nothing.

She goes on: 'Well, try to see *her*, this child,' her eyebrows shoot into arrows, as she waits for a name again, 'as an opportunity. Another little girl in your life. A girl!' She claps her hands, just the once. 'You could go to ballet competitions, and have your nails painted together,' she holds hers up so I can see what painted nails look like, 'and then there'll be all the parties and discos and what-not. It'll be lovely for you to have a chance to experience those things. I do hope it works out that way.'

My hands are clenched into fists at my sides.

'Although hopefully,' it's Moirah now, doing the hoping, 'for your sake, her *father* won't get stuck with all the additional expenses! You know, the things you don't have to worry about as much with Mae. The orthodontist's bills, for one. Honestly, I couldn't believe the cost of braces when we first brought Luke for his.'

I listen to them betray my only daughter, hoping that I will move back here and encourage Olivia into my life because they are curious to have her in theirs. The disabled child and her half-sister from the father's affair playing together in front of their bay windows.

Fantasising about it will keep them going for days.

'And speaking of expense, do you remember how I had the parquet flooring replaced? Just before you left?' A pause for recognition from me. None comes. 'Oh, you do! Saoirse had hers done, and then I decided to?'

I don't care about Anna or her flooring, which makes it difficult to remember. She tuts, and carries on bleating about it anyway. I stop listening. Her words slide past.

I don't want the things that she wants.

I won't live here again, in our giant square house, among the tasteful flower arrangements and the wickedness that comes of living every day without any purpose other than watching to see what others have, what others are doing with their time, with their money. Watching from inside the lines.

'And Mae, of course,' she says. I tune back in for a moment, hearing my daughter's name. 'Now you'll have to find a school that will agree to take her. So much to be done! You might just be in time for this year's deadline for special-needs assistance. There is a Down's boy in one of the mixed schools at the bottom of the hill and I overheard his mother saying how difficult . . .'

She goes on and on, like a loose thread that might be pulled for ever. Her words swim around me and I have to leave. I have to get out of here, out of this conversation. So I say that. 'I have to leave.'

'Oh! What a shame!' Moirah now. 'I was about to suggest we continue this over a—'

'I really have to leave now.' I don't say why.

And I leave the conversation, and I leave Vesey Hill. Leave these two fantasy witches to conspire.

I pull away from the grass verge quickly. They watch me. Their mouths are moving.

Since Sommer moved out and moved on last year, I've no friends here so I've none to lose. I won't need to come through these gates again. I have seen it all.

Mae and I will stay with my father.

Daughters need their fathers.

* * *

I'm making dinner in my dead mother's kitchen. Mae is curled on the cushioned bench by the side door, her legs bent somewhere beneath her, the oil heater at her back.

I think about Steve as I cook, about his phone call earlier this evening. His voice was different. Quieter. Sad, maybe.

'Beth, hi. It's me.'

'Hi. Everything okay?'

'Yeah. So, how was your day?'

'Good. I—'

'Where are you?'

'Home. My dad's.'

'My day was okay, I suppose. It's colder, though, do you think? The place was freezing when I got in from work.'

It was sadness. I hear it now, on replaying the

conversation in my head, a gentle sorrow around his words.

'Maybe a little.'

'It's to be fine tomorrow, though, I think.'

'Steve, I really – I can't do this, I'm sorry. It's too soon, for me. This kind of chat thing. Weather and what-not. You know? I'm not through to the other side of us already, where this doesn't feel weird. It's too little, and it's too much, this small talk.'

'Yeah, sorry. I know. It's just that –' an intake of breath '– I was thinking about things.'

'Okay.'

'About you. About losing you. About the mess I've made.'

'Look, it wasn't just you. Really. We both played a part. A lot of the damage had been done years ago.'

'Okay. That's good, I think. I mean, it's good that you don't just blame me. Although I do – blame myself, I mean.'

He'd paused, and I knew he was choosing his words, picking the best ones. 'I've nothing now. I've nothing without you, Beth.' Picking the bleak ones.

I closed my eyes. He went on, filling the silences, the spaces where my side of the conversation should have been.

'If we could just meet and sit down and really—'

'I'm actually heading out soon so—'

'Oh, sorry. I'll let you go so. But maybe call me later, when you're back from—'

'Steve, honestly. I don't think that's a good idea. Why do you want me to call you later?'

'Just, you know, to talk. When you're back. In. I really miss you, Beth. I think we could—'

'I can't, Steve. You're feeling low right now and I'm sorry for that, but it's just habit that makes us turn to each other when we're down like this. You and me. And then things get more confused, worse. For me, anyway.'

'Oh, right. Okay. If that's—'

'We need to try to be good parents and get our heads straight, not make more of a mess.'

'You're probably right. I'm just struggling, without you.'

I felt myself take a step away from him, from this. From this interest, this sadness brought on, most likely, by coming home to a cold, empty flat. It felt thin and predictable. If he had more of himself to offer, something real and lasting – but he'll most likely master the timer on the heating and fight another day.

Was he always this way? Did I always pump air into him, into us? Keep him buoyant? Buff over the damage?

'Anyway, the kids? Mae, I mean,' he corrects himself quickly. 'How was her day?'

'Good. She's good. Look, I really need to go.'

'Of course. You have plans. We'll talk tomorrow. Have a nice evening – out, wherever you're going. Bye, Bethy.'

'Get your heating organised there and stay warm, okay? Bye, Steve.'

I do miss him, as I'm standing here cooking for the

three of us – Mae, my father and me. What's as easy and what's as impossible as loving one person for life?

* * *

I return Steve's call. The next day. I can tell by his tone that he's not alone. His voice is now that of a man wearing a suit. He says he can't recall what he'd been phoning about. But he'll come back to me 'ASAP'.

My years in New Zealand seem illusory already. A time that could never have lasted. The happiness, the peace. The palette of our life there was bright and simple, because I ignored our darker colours. I didn't have the full picture.

* * *

Mae is eight today. It is 17 January.

There is an ice-cream cake, and Steve comes around, and we all sing 'Happy Birthday' and smile and behave as we should.

'You sounded just like your mother then,' my father says, when I finish the hip-hip-hoorays. Then he clears his throat and picks up the newspaper, rattling it noisily.

Spring is doing its best. The flowerbeds will be expecting my mother soon, if they're not already. Her green leather gardening gloves with the lilac turn-ups and her kneeling mat.

She has been dead for four weeks.

Every morning, I go into the sitting room as soon as I get up. This is where she slept towards the end. I imagine the air is heavy with her, with her life and her death. I go to the windows, frosted with the delicate flowering of the previous night's cold, and I open them, giving them a good shove. Every time, there's a peeling sound and then a release – a seal being broken. I need to let her out, to give her her freedom. But this morning, for the first time, I feel nothing in the room's trapped air. No further sense of her lingering. I pull the blinds right to the top and look out, look up at the sky, expecting to see . . . I don't know what.

She has managed to move out, to move on.

I'm alive and I can't seem to do either of those things.

I'm using my old keys to this house. I bought a new key-ring for them, a black leather B. I coiled the faded plastic heart off the link and threw it into the bin. The alarm code is what it's been all my life – my mother's birthday. We're keeping it, my father and I. It means we still have to think of her every time we come through the door. She'd like that. I like it too.

I set all the clocks to the right time. As a result my father is a few minutes late for an appointment. It will take a little while to adjust to living in the present.

* * *

Sometimes a memory assaults me. Steve saying her name aloud for the first time. *Olivia*. A missile shot into the air, turning, dropping to explode the ground we stood on.

Occasionally, I can't make out if they are actual memories – if the things I remember are real or just imagined. Steve's hand on Jane's thigh. I wasn't there for that, so it can't be a memory, just an image pictured so often that I've managed to deceive my brain. Torturing myself. Justifying everything that's happened since.

* * *

Steve lives in an old apartment with enough rooms for each of his children should they all visit at the same time.

It's spacious and was probably once very beautiful but is worn now, needing attention. Shadows and leaks stain the high ceilings and walls. The sash windows resist any movement along their timber tracks.

'It will give me something to do, restoring it to a former glory,' he said, showing me around. 'Keep me off the streets.'

We both smiled at this.

Over the last few weeks, the restoration has given him something to pay someone else to do, while he works long hours re-establishing himself at the Dublin branch of his firm.

So far, Mae has stayed overnight with him twice.

He doesn't want us to sell the house at Vesey Hill. Because of the property market, he says. He phones me most days now and we talk, plainly but briefly. About our children, about finances. He will arc over the rest of my life and, mostly, I'm glad enough about that.

Of course, the *grá* remains. The love.

He tells me that he and Al have spoken on the phone a few times since we left New Zealand. And he tells me about his father, about Bill, who is still managing to get to Mass.

I don't ask about anyone else.

* * *

I wear my mother's wedding ring. My own is in a velvet box upstairs. My father and I love her fully and openly now she's gone. He and I move around each other, neither of us quite sure what to talk about unless it's her. We always go back to her. She was the doer. The soul of this house. We can see that now.

He has never cooked in his life. Never wants to. He goes to the golf club a lot, has lunch there.

I am a daughter again. I have something ready for him to eat when he gets back.

I am also the woman in this family. I don't ask who he saw. I let him tell me the parts he wants to.

He chats to Mae. She sits up beside him on the couch and he tells her stories. She embraces him, smiles into his tired face, presses her nose to his. She has always known how to be.

* * *

The hooks make a scraping sound moving in their line as my father pulls back the curtains, inviting in the little light that February brings.

'I don't know if I've ever really felt loneliness before,' he says. 'I felt pain when you went away, you and the children. But this is different – this is paralysing. This absolute hollowness. Did I make your mother feel that way, do you think? I know she felt lonely with me – she told me, years ago, when I still listened to her – and I wake up now thinking about that. Beth, do you think your mother lived a lonely life because of me?'

He speaks quietly, but his panic is audible.

'I've always hated this time of year here, Dad. The dark anti-climax of it. The slide from Christmas and New Year into this lengthy, desolate nothing. Listening for spring. I'll probably always hate it more now.'

That's what I say in response to his question.

It's the only honest thing I can think of to fill the silence, falling somewhere between saying nothing and getting into everything.

Something essential in my father is waning, the boldness of his colours leaching from him. I'd always thought he'd know what to do in life, what would happen next. But he doesn't. And is it terrible to think, to know, that I prefer him like this? This uncertain version, having to find his way. This Dad.

* * *

This weekend is Steve's scheduled trip to see Olivia. '"London Calling",' he says, then hums the chorus to me down the phone.

* * *

The evenings are still dark and I listen to the wind, loud and threatening. But this house I grew up in, this house I am growing up in again, feels strong and sturdy against it.

I speak to Al every other night. I am his mother, and I won't be giving that up. I spin the globe and put my finger

251

on Ireland. I imagine tunnelling straight through the orb and out the opposite side, breaking ground in the Pacific Ocean, near New Zealand. I feel the distance as a physical loss. But I'm proud too. My adult son, a man, running his own show.

'I'd love to be there with you, darling. You, me and Mae together,' I say. And then I speak again: 'And your dad. Who knows? Maybe we'll all be able to come and see you sometime, have a few weeks, the four of us.'

Al's wide smile fills the screen.

* * *

Sometimes, for a moment, I catch myself wanting to stretch out and feel a man's hands, a man's arms around me, under me. Arms like Steve's.

To be kissed. Proper kisses – deep and slow. Life has thrilled me before, and I'm hopeful that it will again.

But then I imagine a casual relationship and wonder if such a thing is even possible at my age. Being casual, being passionate with someone when turning fifty is up ahead, with everything that you know. About life. About people.

No new man will ever know the version of me that isn't a mother. Me. Before I had Al, before Mae. Me. Before one child grew up, before Mae. Me. With one gone, one to stay.

Nothing casual about it.

* * *

Mae is what I have left. In a sense, we have nothing – she and I – so we have been liberated. Our house rented out and our men tangled in their own branches, we are two hot-air balloons, our binding cords having come undone.

Here, both of us in hats and scarves on the sand at Dún Laoghaire, her arm hooked through mine, I feel both lost and found. She looks happy, so I know she is. And I think this must be it, that this will be our home. I will get a little place for us here by the wild Irish Sea. A little place for a bigger life.

And once I make this decision, my spirit responds and catches the waves, rises for a moment, then falls.

And rises again.

Time. The Healer.

Two months later

I bump into Steve on the street. Just him, the man. Not separated-from-me Steve or weekend-dad Steve, just him.

There is no handover detail about what time our daughter last ate, no overnight instructions, no bag for her gymnastics class in the morning. Nothing to watch for, nothing to report.

Seeing him out of our context like this throws me off kilter. Or on kilter. Whichever means that everything in my day suddenly tilts a different way, but is so much brighter for it.

We are in Dublin city in the April sunshine, the coloured doors of Georgian buildings catching our light. The man I once fell for and me. And it feels like a tiny party. An afternoon party for two, with joy and attraction pouring from us both.

And we talk and we laugh and we smile, and our exchanges are free and uncomplicated, and somewhere in the honesty of being caught unawares and unrehearsed and alone on the pavement, he kisses me. This man.

And I kiss him back.

And every good feeling I've ever had for us seems to waken and rise and bubble up inside me, making it as much a cry-out as a kiss.

But, oh, it's everything – a miraculous picking up of the best that we were and might be, with knowledge of the worst. It's impulse and it's heart.

And all the trouble and the envy and the mistrust don't scorch us as we stand here, caught up as we are in the waves of our joy and our recognition of each other.

And I am sobbing, and then we both are. Sobbing and laughing and snotting and wiping and smiling, and it doesn't feel like a making-do, or a habit. It feels like love.

Love, but with our eyes open. With the dark colours, as well as the bright.

Our tears and our laughter settle, and then my head is against his chest, my cheek on his heart. We both say that we remember how lovely the other can be.

And what's between us is so complete right now, is so clear and loud, that it mutes any life we've had apart over the last few months. In his arms I find that my memories of warm days by the sea recline intact.

Maybe one unspoiled moment is all it takes. For an

astonishing clarity that allows both of you to let the fear go, to let the pretence go, and to say yes.

Yes to love.

Yes to Al and Mae, and yes to Olivia.

Yes to strength in numbers.

We are at home with each other, and we will make our own weather.

Acknowledgements

Thanks to Ciara Doorley and Joanna Smyth at Hachette Ireland for supporting me, to Yvonne Cullen and Noelle Harrison for reading for me, to Ruth for listening to me, to Matthew for giving me time, and to New Zealand for having me.

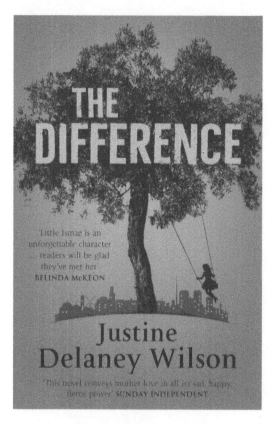

The Difference

On a January morning, Beth and Steve bring three-day-old
Ismae home from the hospital. A little girl to complete
their suburban family.

Except Beth knows that Ismae is different. And that, as she gets
older and stronger, her difference will become more obvious.

As the future Beth imagined grows even more out of reach, the
walls of their vast house close in on her, isolating her from Steve.

Then she makes a terrible discovery ...

Will Ismae's difference break her family apart? Or will Beth be
able to see that it's the one thing that can save her?

Also available as an ebook